Murder at the Tea Party

1920s Historical Cozy Mystery

An Evie Parker Mystery

SONIA PARIN

ISBN: 9781796232141

1
Home Sweet Home

Late Spring 1920
Halton House, Berkshire
The Countess of Woodridge's country estate

"Caro, at some point, I might need to call upon you to be my alibi."

Her maid gave a small, barely perceptible nod but didn't comment.

Evie watched Caro fussing with her hair and tried to determine if she had said something to upset her. She stopped short of declaring she would parade through the village in the way Lady Godiva had because she suspected Caro's response would be an insouciant shrug...

Since arriving at Halton House late the previous evening, Evie had been distracted but not enough to miss Caro's odd behavior. She couldn't remember her usually chatty maid ever looking so tight-lipped. Evie would almost go so far as to say her maid sported a look of disapproval.

"Will you be needing a hat today, milady?" Caro asked.

"Yes, please. I'm meeting the estate agent and we're going out for an early morning walk around the estate. I'd like to meet and greet as many tenants as I can during my stay. After a two-year absence, they've probably forgotten who I am or what I even look like. I might be hauled away as a trespasser."

Normally, such a remark would have produced a chuckle out of Caro but her lips remained pursed.

"Caro, is there something worrying you?"

"No, milady. I'm perfectly fine." Her maid drew in a sharp breath. "The same can't be said for a little seven-year-old boy forced to attend boarding school at such a tender age."

Ah… She had to be referring to Seth Halton. Her late husband's heir and current Earl of Woodridge. "It's called a preparatory school. There's nothing unusual about it. In fact, it's quite acceptable for someone of his rank to spend his formative years at boarding school."

Caro didn't seem to agree.

"Don't you think he's too young? He should be out and about, getting into scrapes…"

"You forget who he is, Caro. I don't have the skills or appropriate experience to bring him up. Besides, he was quite looking forward to it."

Caro harrumphed. "That's because he wanted to get away from his tutors. Both Mr. Hurlington and Mr. Swindon are so severe looking, I wouldn't be surprised if poor Seth had been suffering from night terrors."

"There's nothing poor about Seth," Evie murmured under her breath. Her late husband, Nicholas Halton, had been an astute landowner and investor, always thinking of the future. His estate continued to pay for itself and, because of his cautious guiding hand, would continue to do so for many generations to come.

A knock at the door preceded the butler's entrance. "My lady, there is a telegram for you."

"Thank you, Edgar." Evie took the piece of paper and unfolded it with the eagerness of someone who'd been expecting news from abroad. Reading the message, she pressed her hand to her throat.

"I hope it's not bad news, my lady."

"No, Edgar. It isn't." At least not for her... However, she would have to deal with a very delicate matter.

For a moment, Evie considered keeping the information to herself. Leaving the decision until later, she set the telegram aside and smiled at Edgar. "How are you enjoying being away from London?"

She could tell Edgar had a great deal to say about taking up the role of butler at the country estate but her snooty butler would reserve his opinions. No matter how much she invited him to open up, he always abided by the less said is better rule.

"It is a rare pleasure to spend a few months in

the country, my lady."

Oh, yes. She would not have expected less than a well measured response. Edgar would definitely excel in the diplomatic arena, Evie thought. Basically, his remark suggested he would much rather avoid the country but would suffer a brief visit, enduring it in absolute silence because it would be improper and impolite to remark upon her ladyship's decisions.

"Thank you for stepping in, Edgar. Mr. Crawford appreciates you helping out during his hour of need. I hear his sister is on the mend but we should be generous and allow him to spend some extra time with her."

"As you wish, my lady."

Evie waited for Edgar to withdraw before taking another look at the telegram.

"Have you seen Tom?" she asked Caro.

"No, milady. After your arrival yesterday, he made himself scarce."

How would he react to the news? Did he already know? Maybe that's why he'd made himself scarce, Evie thought.

Several weeks back, she'd felt she had made some headway with her chauffeur. Tom Winchester had proven to be a surprise package with his ability to blend in almost anywhere, playing the role of Mr. Winchester, self-made man about town, to the hilt and without a single fault.

Unforeseen circumstances had taken care of

wrenching away the social barriers that had been standing between them and Evie had enjoyed their even playing field but it hadn't lasted. As soon as they had left the Duke of Hetherington's house, Tom had reverted to his monosyllabic responses and, instead of continuing to call her Evie, he had resumed referring to her as ma'am but only because she had forbidden him to call her my lady. To think she'd had to threaten him with a one-way ticket back to Boston…

"Will that be all, milady?"

"Caro, you can't possibly still be cross with me. Trust me, it is customary for young boys to be sent to boarding school."

"Yes, of course… I suppose…" Caro shrugged. "I think I entertained a few fanciful ideas about you taking him under your wing."

In an ideal world, Evie thought it might have been possible. But she still had her own wounds to deal with. Her husband had only been gone for two years. The moment she thought she'd overcome her loss, she found herself wanting to share something with him…

How many times had she turned, laughing at some silly remark someone had made and wishing to share it only to suddenly remember he wasn't there to hear her?

"The poor little mite," Caro continued. "He doesn't have any family."

"Seth will be making lifelong friends at school," Evie offered. "You really needn't worry about him. In years to come, everyone he meets now will be attending house parties and balls at Halton House." Evie went to stand in front of the mirror to inspect the ensemble Caro had selected for her. "I'll need to see Mrs. Arnold later today to discuss the menus for the week. Could you please remind her?"

Caro nodded. "Will you be lunching here today, milady?"

Evie tilted her head from side to side. Caro had a particular talent for matching the colors of her clothes and she'd never had reason to question her attention to detail. However, something didn't look quite right.

Evie narrowed her gaze and scrutinized her reflection. "No, I think I'll walk into the village and see what I can find there."

"You'll have to remember to return in time for afternoon tea with the dowagers," Caro reminded her.

Evie stilled. She had forgotten. "It's just as well Seth is so young and unmarried, otherwise… I'd be a dowager too."

Afternoon tea with the Most Honorable, the Dowager Countess of Woodridge. Two of them. Nicholas's mother and grandmother.

Upon her arrival at Halton House, she had been surprised to find they had both moved out and into the dower house nearby. She supposed she would hear all about the reasons why they had taken such a hasty course of action because...

"Ours is not to reason why," Evie murmured and added, "they're probably trying to make a point." Although, she suspected it would be up to her to unravel the message.

Her relationship with her husband's family had been smooth sailing from the start, but only because she had chosen to turn a blind eye. Of course, there had been hints of disappointment because Nicholas Halton, Earl of Woodridge had fallen in love with a foreigner instead of one of their own, but Evie had been sensible enough to appeal to their better natures. Instead of choosing to do everything her way, she had placed her destiny in their hands, making it clear she could not possibly do the job without their knowledgeable guidance.

Evie adjusted her hat, tilting it to one side and then the other. It really did look odd but she couldn't quite put her finger on it. Then, on closer inspection, she noticed the bunch of little flowers had all the petals plucked out.

Looking askance, Caro gave her an impish smile and handed her another hat. "Try this one, milady."

"Oh, much better." Evie gave her maid a small smile. "If I didn't know better, I'd think you'd taken out your frustration on the poor petals."

Caro's cheeks flushed a delicate shade of pink and she whispered, "He is only seven."

***

Meet and greet

"Hollyhock Farm is up ahead," the estate agent said, his tone distracted.

Mr. Gregory Wellington had met Evie at the doorstep. While she had looked forward to a walk, he had insisted on driving her to the nearest farms, saying he only had limited time to spend on the tour.

Evie found herself saying, "I really don't wish to impose on your schedule. Perhaps I could trek out alone and leave you to it."

But he wouldn't hear of it. Either because he didn't find it appropriate for the lady of the house to wander around unaccompanied or because he considered the local tenants his responsibility and he didn't want the Countess of Woodridge imposing on his territory.

As the motor car came to a stop, she looked ahead and saw another car disappearing down the narrow road. A chauffeur driven car. She couldn't think of any reason why such a car would be driving out this way…

She turned her attention to the farm and hollyhocks growing in abundance. "Oh, I see why it's called Hollyhock Farm. I've never seen so many of them planted in the same place, but isn't it early for blooms?"

The agent gave a shrug. "I believe the tenant excels at greenhouse planting."

Evie found the idea intriguing. They had a small greenhouse at Halton House. She didn't know the first thing about gardening but with so many people engaged to maintain the estate, she might be able to find someone willing to give her basic instructions. The more she thought about it, the more interested she became in finding something other than embroidery to engage her attention for a few hours…

Glancing down the road again, Evie saw the car had now disappeared. She couldn't help wondering what they might have been doing out this way. "What's the tenant's name?"

"Charlie Timms. His family has been farming here for over a hundred years."

The man himself strode out to greet them and showed them through to his stables saying, "We diversified and introduced a stud farm and breeding program a couple of years ago at the Earl's suggestion and it has paid dividends, my lady. His lordship's input is sorely missed."

Evie couldn't help noticing Charlie Timms was a bit of a stud himself. Tall with broad shoulders, his easy smile spoke of friendliness. When he directed a remark at Evie, his tone lightened and his smile reached all the way to his eyes.

"We best keep moving, my lady," the agent suggested.

After an hour, Evie realized the agent wanted to get through the tour as quickly as possible, which made her wonder if he really did disapprove of her attempt to become better acquainted with the tenants. A subject best left for another day, she thought as she slipped her hand inside her pocket. Feeling the folded piece of paper, she realized today would be a day of postponing all major decisions for no other reason than to avoid treading on anyone's toes.

"You can drop me off here," she said when they reached the village. "I'll be happy to stretch my legs and make my own way back to Halton House." And next time, she thought, she would pay everyone a visit on her own and have some relevant questions to ask. Now that she'd returned to England and to Halton House, she wanted to start making some sort of headway with her life. And that, she knew, meant she had to show an interest.

Had to or wanted to?

Giving a small nod of approval, Evie decided she wanted to take an interest. She already felt everything beginning to fall into place, almost as if she had been in a dream and had only now woken up to face the reality of life. One simply needed to get on with it.

She couldn't fault the agent's ability to perform his job but his brisk manner had impeded her attempt to establish herself as a familiar figure in the area.

Another nod confirmed her decision to do something about that…

From a distance, she spotted a sign written in elegant script right above the picture of an enticing looking pie.

Mrs. Baker's Delights

"A new addition," she mused. When she reached the tea room, she peered through the window and smiled. This hadn't been here the last time she'd visited the small village of Halton. There were several tables covered with white tablecloths and adorned with pretty bouquets of wild flowers. Seeing a waitress stride by with a tray of dainty pies enticed Evie inside the tea room.

The moment she stepped inside, she heard someone murmur her name. She saw a group of women sitting at a table huddling together as if to exchange what information they had about her.

"A table by the window, please," she said when the waitress approached her.

"Certainly, milady. This way, please."

Happy with her choice because it offered a perfect view of the village as well as every table in the small establishment, Evie perused the menu. "This sounds delicious. Game pie."

"Excellent choice, milady. It is one of our most popular pies."

Evie smiled at the young waitress. "And some tea, please."

Moments later, the waitress returned. "Begging your pardon, milady. The ladies from the Hunt Ball Committee wonder if you would do them the honor of joining them at their table."

A committee? She couldn't remember the Hunt Ball ever having a committee… Also, she hadn't participated in one of those since… Well, since she'd left England. She supposed now that she'd returned there would be no more shirking off the responsibilities expected of her. There would be flower shows and fundraisers, tea parties and luncheons. Everything the dowagers would have been taking care of during her absence.

Had the dowagers moved out of the main house because she'd now returned and they didn't wish to overshadow her role as the current Countess of Woodridge? Evie had always been only too happy to share the spotlight. However, she knew their opinions on the matter would differ greatly.

"Yes, of course. I'd love to join them. It would be my pleasure." Evie braced herself for the encounter. When she reached the table, she found a familiar face.

The Vicar's wife, Mrs. Ellington straightened and smiled. "Lady Woodridge. You honor us," the Vicar's wife said and proceeded to make the introductions.

Evie sat between Mrs. Howard-Smith, married to an Earl's youngest son, and Mrs.

Penn, married to a solicitor.

She smiled at the two ladies sitting opposite her; Mrs. Browning, married to the village doctor, and Mrs. Hallesberry, married to a local landowner.

"We've been discussing the upcoming Hunt Ball," Mrs. Ellington said. "It seems ages since you last attended."

Evie didn't know if she needed to apologize to the Vicar's wife for her absence or offer detailed explanations. Seeing everyone leaning forward slightly, she decided they were interested in what she had been up to.

Half way through recounting some of her adventures in New York and Newport, most of which had already faded with nothing much of significance to remember, they all turned their attention to a newcomer. Evie could not have been more relieved by the interruption as the questions had invariably focused on how she had managed to survive without her husband.

"She looks like a flapper," Mrs. Penn remarked, her tone holding a mixture of disapproval and admiration.

"Or one of the bright young things I've been hearing so much about," Mrs. Ellington whispered with a degree of excitement in her voice.

Having held many laborious conversations with the Vicar, Evie understood his wife's possible yearning for some fun.

The young woman in question sat down at the table Evie had vacated only moments before. She cast her eyes around the tea room, the edge of her lip lifted either in appreciation, disdain or amusement for what the small village had to offer. Meanwhile, her presence held everyone at the table enthralled, and with good reason. She wore a man's suit and the most outrageous trousers Evie had ever seen with pink and gray stripes.

"She must be new or passing through," the Vicar's wife said. "I certainly don't recognize her." Turning back to Evie, she asked, "Will you be here long enough to attend the Hunt Ball? It's in a month's time."

As Evie answered in the affirmative, she noticed their attention shifting again. One by one, they looked out toward the window and the street beyond.

"Now there's a sight for sore eyes," the doctor's wife said.

Recognizing the man who stopped briefly by the tea room window, Evie smiled with interest as, clearly, the ladies were all agog over the sight of the local tenant farmer she had labeled a stud. She watched their eyes glazing over, their lips parting slightly. To her amusement, none of them appeared to be blinking.

When Charlie Timms tipped his hat at someone and strode away, it took several minutes for everyone to recover. Evie didn't want to jump to conclusions but his departure appeared to have left the ladies feeling bereft. Two of them sighed. One fanned herself. While the Vicar's wife shifted in her seat, her cheeks coloring with a tinge of pink.

Mrs. Howard-Smith excused herself saying she remembered she had people coming around in a short while and needed to hurry back home but it had been a great pleasure meeting the Countess and she looked forward to seeing her at the Hunt Ball.

Evie expected everyone to resume their conversation. Instead, they all fell silent. A sense of awkwardness gripped her. If her lunch hadn't arrived, she might have made an excuse to leave. Even with the enticing pie sitting in front of her, she considered finding any excuse to bid the ladies goodbye and head on home, but the pie looked too good to miss out on.

As she took the first bite, she noticed something else. She had become the object of the new arrival's interest. It worked both ways. Evie didn't fail to notice the young woman producing a small flask and tipping some of its contents into her teacup. The woman's raised eyebrow either challenged Evie to say something or mocked her for noticing. As Evie held no opinions on the matter, she didn't care either way.

At least, Evie thought, she would have something to talk about when she met the dowagers for afternoon tea…

2
Two dowagers and a Countess walked into a room

Halton House
The Japanese drawing room

Sara, Lady Woodridge lifted the dainty teacup only to set it down again. "You have been gone for so long, we thought you would never return."

"And yet, here I am, mama." Nicholas' mother had always encouraged Evie to address her as mama. It had taken some getting used to, especially as Evie's own mother had always preferred to be addressed by her first name or, if need be, as mother.

During her walk back from the village, she had made a firm decision to avoid bringing up the subject of the dowagers' unexpected departure from Halton House. If the dowagers wished to make a point, they would have to do so on their own and without any encouragement whatsoever from Evie.

Evie smiled. It would drive them batty. Of course, being a cut to the chase type of person, she knew she would find it difficult to refrain from asking leading questions but she held onto her resolve.

Evie gave Sara her undivided attention, smiling and nodding as she spoke of the events that had taken place during the last couple of years. Sara mentioned the Hunt Ball several times. When she mentioned it again, Evie wondered if it could be a key element to the reason why the dowagers had moved out of the main house. Although, she couldn't see how it would be.

Playing the game of avoidance took so much effort, Evie kept forgetting to mention she had met the Hunt Ball Committee ladies…

After half an hour, and not without a twinge of regret for weakening so soon, she decided to make a slight alteration to her plans. Avoiding the subject Sara clearly wished to tackle by not once referring to it would only drag it out and perhaps even create a rift between them. Something she wished to avoid at all cost.

"I couldn't help noticing you are no longer residing at Halton House."

Sara's breezy manner came as a surprise. "Yes, we thought it might be about time. We felt we had been delaying it for far too long. And now here you are and as we were not sure of your intentions…" Sara gave a small shrug.

Evie leaned forward, held her position for a second and then she settled back. The remark had been meant to lure her into asking for explanations, but she wouldn't. Oh, no… She would not ask.

Edgar strode in, cleared his throat and announced, "The Dowager Countess of Woodridge."

Not for the first time, Evie wondered if butlers were taught to clear their throats before making their announcements.

"Henrietta," Evie exclaimed. "How lovely it is to see you." She set her teacup down and hurried across the room to greet her grandmama. To think she had three of those and each one with their own peculiar and stubborn ways.

Henrietta smiled. "If not for your regular letters, we would have thought you'd gone forever from our lives."

And yet, since her return to England, they had met for luncheon and dinner in London. Several times…

"So, is he here?" Henrietta asked.

Evie did her best to look confused. She didn't have to try very hard because, even after delving deep, she couldn't come up with any other person to whom the dowager might have been referring to.

"Seth? Well, no. He already left for boarding school." Evie gestured toward the sofa and returned to her own chair. She considered telling them about Caro's unique way of expressing her displeasure over the young master's exile to boarding school but decided they might not see the humor in it and would insist she dismiss her maid for insubordination. "Have some tea."

Accepting a cup of tea, Henrietta exchanged a look with Sara that spoke of secret understandings and possible collusion.

"We have been informed of a new presence in your life, dear Evangeline."

The dowagers gazed at her without blinking. Almost as if they didn't dare risk missing out on her reaction.

Evie gave a small shake of her head. "I'm sorry, I'm not sure I understand…"

"News has reached us about a certain Mr. Winchester accompanying you about town."

How exactly had word reached them? She had only been out and about with Tom… or rather, with Mr. Winchester the one time when they had both trekked out from the Duke's Yorkshire house to London in pursuit of some information.

Giving a self-satisfied nod, Henrietta stated, "You were both seen lunching together at the Criterion in Piccadilly Circus."

Evie tried to recall the story they had made up for the benefit of the Duke's guests. Giving them a small smile, she said, "He's a friend from way back. We grew up together and then, we grew apart, as people do. Fortunately, a casual encounter renewed our friendship. After hearing me talk so much about England, he decided to visit."

She thought she heard Sara say something

about Evie never once mentioning him.

"I see," Henrietta said. "And should we expect a visit from him here at Halton House?"

Would the dowagers object? And how would she pull it off? At some point, they were bound to encounter Tom, her chauffeur. "I'm not sure what his plans are."

"So, he is still in England." The dowagers exchanged another glance, its meaning understood by them alone.

"Yes, as far as I know. But that might change at any moment. He's quite a free spirit. Comes and goes on a whim." Evie took a sip of her tea and smiling, asked, "How exactly did news about him reach you?"

"Word gets around, my dear."

Evie tried to determine if Henrietta had meant it as a warning or as a simple statement of fact. Her gaze strayed toward Edgar.

"Oh, no. Don't look at him," Henrietta warned. "Edgar would never betray your confidence."

"How do you know?" Evie asked and wondered if Henrietta knew because she had already tried to extricate information from Edgar.

The dowager pursed her lips and shifted in her seat. "Never fear, we have your best interests at heart."

If not her butler, then who could have passed on the information? Someone else who'd seen them at the restaurant?

"You shouldn't take offence, Edgar," the dowager said to the butler who gave a nod of acknowledgment. "Her ladyship is very guarded about her private life and is bound to want to find out who revealed her secret."

"But it's not exactly a secret," Evie said.

"Then why haven't we heard about Mr. Winchester before? I hope you were not trying to spare our feelings. You are quite young and both Sara and I expect you to find someone with whom to share your life with. It's expected. We wouldn't want you to live a life of seclusion. Speaking of which…" Looking toward the door, Henrietta said, "I have invited someone else to join us for tea."

Sara didn't look surprised so Evie had to assume she had known of this all along.

A footman entered and murmured something to Edgar. Standing at attention, he announced, "Mrs. Penn."

Henrietta welcomed Mrs. Penn and gestured to the chair beside her. "Oh, I beg your pardon, Evangeline. Old habits and all that… Of course, you might not have met Mrs. Penn as she is relatively new to our little village. She is married to a local solicitor."

The solicitor's wife settled opposite Evie.

Evie smiled at her. "Lovely to see you again, Mrs. Penn."

"Oh, please call me Clarissa," Mrs. Penn

offered.

"You've met?" Henrietta could not have sounded more surprised.

Evie nodded. "I had lunch at Mrs. Baker's Delights today and was invited to join some ladies. The group included the Vicar's wife."

Henrietta exchanged another look with Sara. This time, they shared a lengthy, wordless conversation.

Evie called on all her patience and decided all would be revealed in time.

"How interesting. Did they happen to mention the Hunt Ball?" Henrietta asked.

"As a matter of fact, yes. It's coming up soon and I am quite looking forward to attending. It's one of my favorite events."

Henrietta set her teacup down. "And did it not strike you as odd that a group of local women would be discussing the Hunt Ball without either Sara or myself present?"

"Oh, now that you mention it, yes." She had wondered about the existence of a committee but her curiosity had not progressed from there. "I must admit I didn't give it much thought."

"Well, here's something for you to think about. Those women have absconded with our ball," the dowager huffed out her indignation. "They pulled the rug from right under us. Sara and I have been doing our outmost to remain civil but it is extremely hard to do so when there are mutineers among us."

Evie risked a glance at Clarissa Penn who appeared to be unaffected by the dowager's remarks.

"Oh, you needn't worry about Clarissa. She's actually one of us."

The plot thickens, Evie thought.

Henrietta leaned forward and lowered her voice, "She is our spy."

Evie's eyebrows curved upward as she mouthed the word. "Spy?"

Henrietta nodded. "She offered."

"To what end?" Evie asked, her tone sounding as naïve as she felt.

"Well, we can't just leave it at that. They have no right to even presume to think they can organize such an event. It has always been headed by a Woodridge. In fact, we pay for it all and even hold it here at Halton House. I cannot begin to tell you how deeply disappointed I am with Mrs. Ellington. You would think the Vicar's wife would remain neutral. No, indeed. In fact, it was all her idea, I'm sure of it. She single-handedly organized the munity and now you tell us she invited you to join her group for lunch." Henrietta looked at Sara. They both nodded and then Henrietta said to Evie, "She's going to try to get you on side because she realizes she needs a Woodridge to legitimize her project."

"More tea?" Evie offered and wished she could have something stronger.

"Do I hear you ask how it happened?"

Henrietta asked.

"Sara, would you like more tea," Evie offered.

"No, I'm fine, dear."

"And you, Clarissa?" Evie didn't wait for her to reply. "Edgar, please refresh Mrs. Penn's tea." Turning back to Clarissa, she said, "It's my own special blend. I never thought I'd acquire a taste for tea but, here I am, quite addicted." Noticing Henrietta giving her a pointed look, Evie apologized. "Do go on."

"Well," Henrietta continued. "There we were, getting on like a house on fire when Mrs. Ellington suggested we had been doing things our way for far too long."

Evie took a moment to get her thoughts into some sort of order. Setting her cup down, Evie asked, "How did Mrs. Ellington and the others become involved?" After all, as Henrietta had pointed out, the Hunt Ball was a Woodridge tradition.

Henrietta gave an unladylike snort. "By nefarious means but more on that later. As I was saying… Had she made suggestions, we might have reached some sort of compromise. Instead, she proposed a vote for a change of leadership saying we would do better if we allowed a more democratic selection of the committee. Can you believe we would ever experience such dissent among the ranks?"

Evie tried to come up with a noncommittal answer. It wouldn't do to take sides even though she knew she would be required to do so. "Had the Vicar's wife expressed dissatisfaction with the way you organized the event?" she asked.

"No. Never. Certainly not within my hearing," Henrietta said. "That made it that much more surprising when she finally launched her rebellion. I strongly believe she has been influenced by Mrs. Howard-Smith. She is quite an upstart and behaves as such."

Deciding she needed to hear all the details, Evie said, "I think you really need to explain why the Vicar's wife and the others became involved."

Sara placed a staying hand on the dowager and smiled as she said, "Do you remember how we had to postpone the event during the war?"

Oh, yes. Halton House had been turned into a convalescent home for soldiers recovering from their injuries.

"Well," Sara continued, "if you recall, at the end of the war, we continued to serve as a convalescent home for a lot longer than other houses. And then we also incorporated rehabilitation for the most unfortunate souls who'd lost limbs."

Evie nodded. In reality, she had switched off. Nicholas had died a few months before the war had ended. Every day had been a reminder of what she'd lost. Yet, she'd had to soldier on. Until she could no longer fake it. Devastated by her loss and utterly ashamed at not being able to carry on, she had fled back home to America…

Sara continued, "A few months after the war ended, someone mentioned the Hunt Ball and how it would be a wonderful opportunity to raise some much-needed funds for the local hospital. Henrietta and I were both delighted by the idea but we couldn't bring ourselves to turn out all those soldiers in need. So, the Vicar's wife suggested holding the event at Witford Hall. We celebrated its huge success. That was last year." Sara concluded her tale by saying, "Now, we are back to normal and so we assumed the ball would be back where it belongs."

Henrietta gave a stiff nod. "The Vicar's wife chose her moment well. When the ball had been held at Witford Hall, Mrs. Ellington gathered together a few women and offered to assist with the planning. We welcomed and encouraged her involvement because Sara and I had been so busy we didn't think we would find the time to trek out to Witford Hall. It's about ten odd miles from here and it would have been too time consuming to oversee the preparations ourselves. Anyhow, that was then, this is now. Once we decided to resume all the annual activities at Halton House, Mrs. Ellington somehow talked her way in by saying we had done so much for the war effort, it would be unfair to leave us to our own devices. We didn't want to seem ungrateful…"

Sara nodded. "Also, the Vicar's wife made a valid point. If something were to happen to either

Henrietta or myself… If either one of us fell ill, it would make sense to have someone step in. After all, we had decided to continue on with the idea of raising funds which makes the event that much more significant."

Henrietta cut in, saying, "Little did we know the Vicar's wife had a plan in place. She had been most cunning in getting others, including Mrs. Howard-Smith, on side and inviting them to join our little group. To this day, I suspect Mrs. Howard-Smith may well be behind all this. They began by finding fault with everything we proposed. Finally, they suggested the ball would be better served at Witford Hall. At least, for the time being."

Evie remembered the lady in question had been present at lunch. "I take it Mrs. Howard-Smith has some influence over the owners of Witford Hall."

Henrietta harrumphed. "I'll say she does since she is married to the owner. Edward Howard-Smith. He's the youngest son of the Earl of Rosenthal. The year we couldn't hold the ball at Halton House they offered the use of their house but then the Countess fell ill. That's when the Vicar's wife suggested Witford Hall."

"Oh… Has the Countess of Rosenthal recovered?" Evie asked.

"She has, although you wouldn't know it by the way she carries on. One moment she is at death's door and the next, she is out and about riding. I have seen her with my own eyes. And yes, I am about to suggest she is in collusion with her daughter-in-law, Mrs. Howard-Smith, who has been kicking up a fuss about making a name for herself in the district. Apparently, she aspires to become a prominent social hostess. Evidently, by brute force."

"I don't quite understand. Why didn't they simply set up their own event?" Evie asked and watched as the dowagers gazed at her in admiration. Later, Evie would realize they had been in awe of her naivety.

"Because Mrs. Howard-Smith wishes to have her way." Henrietta turned to Clarissa. "Tell her what you told me earlier on."

Clarissa had been about to take a bite of cake. Urged by the dowager, she set the tasty morsel down. "Mrs. Howard-Smith intends to claim exclusive rights to hold the ball every year. She put that at the top of today's agenda."

Henrietta declared, "I say we mount an offensive attack and hold our own ball. Not an alternative one but rather the one and only Hunt Ball."

"But won't that cause more problems?" Evie asked. "Surely there is an amicable way around it all."

"They have thrown down the gauntlet," Henrietta clipped out in her most indignant tone. "To the victor go the spoils and I aim to be victorious."

3
Fences to mend

Halton House

“Mrs. Howard-Smith,” Edgar announced.

Evie gave the rebel a warm welcome. “Thank you for coming at such short notice.”

“My apologies for being late,” Mrs. Howard-Smith offered. “We held another Hunt Ball Committee meeting today and I’m afraid it went on for longer than expected. So many details to take care of, and so little time to do it in.”

Evie had, on occasion, heard whispered remarks about her brashness. She had always felt the observations had failed to take into account the reality of the matter. Yes, she sounded different but she also held her own opinions. And, being American should not, in her opinion, instantly label her as being brash.

After her first encounter with Mrs. Howard-Smith and even after Henrietta’s harsh assessment of the woman’s concentrated effort to debunk her from her social position, Evie would not have described Mrs. Howard-Smith as being brash.

However, judging by the tone employed to explain her tardiness, she would quite happily and without any reservations whatsoever declare the woman to be utterly and without any shame quite brash.

She might even go so far as to say Mrs. Howard-Smith had flaunted her involvement in the Hunt Ball. In fact, she would make sure her report to the dowagers included the precise description of the woman's attitude.

Without a doubt, it had been brazenly arrogant.

"How lovely it is to see you again. Won't you come through?" Evie led her to the small drawing room; one of several rooms in the house designed specifically for the lady of the house to entertain small parties.

"This is such a delightful room," Mrs. Howard-Smith said.

"Thank you. The Dowager Countess is solely responsible for the decorations. She has exquisite taste." All the chairs in the room were upholstered in pretty floral and pastoral designs of pale green and pink to match the wallpaper.

"And the view of the gardens is magnificent." Mrs. Howard-Smith settled down and held Evie's gaze for a moment. "Is anyone else joining us?"

"No, I thought it might be best if we spoke alone."

Mrs. Howard-Smith gave a knowing nod. "I

see. This is about the Hunt Ball."

"Let's have some tea first." Belatedly, Evie wished she had invited Mrs. Howard-Smith to lunch. A glass of fortifying wine would have been greatly appreciated.

She'd never imagined having to play the role of peacemaker and had no idea how she would go about restoring a sense of harmony and goodwill between everyone involved. A difficult task to tackle, she knew, as there could only be one solution. The Dowager Countess would settle for nothing less than a full admission of guilt, an apology and a swift and humble retreat.

Observing the rituals of tea making, Evie poured some hot water into the teapot, gave the pot a brief swirl and then tipped the water into a small bowl. She spooned in the special blend of tea and, after pouring some hot water, allowed the tea to steep.

"You might find this strange," Evie remarked, "I still consider myself a relative newcomer and even an outsider. When it comes to traditions, I believe in going with the flow. As I've often observed, making any suggestion that involves change requires faultless timing and delicate handling. Otherwise, one risks ruffling feathers and rapturing friendships."

Lifting her chin, Mrs. Howard-Smith asked, "Did the dowager happen to mention how she wished to head the committee and organize the event despite the fact it would be held elsewhere?"

She hadn't. Not really. Evie assumed Mrs. Howard-Smith had been referring to the previous year's event when the Countess of Rosenthal had been taken ill and the event had been held at Witford Hall. In any case, she knew Henrietta would have happily offered to step into the Countess' shoes. So, Evie had to give her the benefit of the doubt and say she had only wished to be of help.

Trying not to frown, Evie also thought the dowager would have been well within her rights to insist on heading the committee.

Upon further reflection, Evie remembered the dowager had claimed Witford Hall had been too far for her to travel to while at the same time overseeing the convalescing activities taking place at Halton House.

Mrs. Howard-Smith had just lied to her…

They managed to get through their first cup of tea and piece of lemon cake when, out of the blue, Mrs. Howard-Smith declared she would not back down, so any efforts to change her mind would be futile.

She also added, "I had rather hoped you would join us, but it seems you wish to remain faithful to the old guard."

Evie could only respond with a slight lift of her eyebrows. She poured herself another cup of tea and, after a restorative sip, she said, "I do wish you would try to meet us half way."

"Us? Us?"

To her dismay, Mrs. Howard-Smith took exception to the remark.

"I really don't need to hear this," Mrs. Howard-Smith stated. "I will not be railroaded into toeing the line. I should have known better than to think you could be an ally. I thought I could trust you."

To do what? Evie couldn't help wondering. Revolt against her own family?

Realizing Evie would not be swayed to join forces with the rebels, Mrs. Howard-Smith erupted to her feet.

Gripping the back of the chair, Mrs. Howard-Smith then concluded by saying, "It's all fine and dandy for you when you've had everything handed in a silver platter. As you can see, your efforts to rein me in have failed. Good day."

A footman hurried to open the door for Mrs. Howard-Smith while Edgar stepped forward to say, "May I have your permission from here onwards to say you are not receiving visitors?"

Evie took a sip of her tea and sighed. "If you wish, Edgar, but I doubt you will have the opportunity. I think Mrs. Howard-Smith has severed all connections with us and has cast us adrift."

"Indeed. But what right has she to do that?" Edgar murmured.

Evie tried to think what she might have said to provoke such an outburst from Mrs. Howard-

Smith. The shock over the woman's abrupt departure still quaked through her when the door opened and Henrietta strode in, or rather, she marched in.

Evie could not have been more surprised.

"Well? Did you give her a piece of your mind?" Henrietta demanded. "If what the footman says is true, I dare say she deserved it."

Had the dowager been lurking in the shadows? A second later, it clicked. "You set me up. You knew I'd contact Mrs. Howard-Smith."

"Yes, of course. You are the voice of calm reason. We actually thought you might bring her around to our point of view but it seems we were wrong."

Evie looked heavenwards. "I doubt anyone can reason with her. She has a major fixation."

"Do tell," the dowager encouraged.

"She practically accused me of having a silver spoon in my mouth. What is her background?"

The dowager rolled her eyes. "Merchandizing of sorts. Her family made their fortune importing cotton fabrics into the country. Or so the story goes. For all we know, they might have been rum smugglers."

Yes, it wouldn't surprise Evie. Mrs. Howard-Smith had certainly displayed a character trait more suited to a brawler than a well brought up woman of substantial means.

"I am sorry I couldn't be of help," Evie offered.

"Oh, don't apologize. I doubt anyone would have been able to reason with the woman." Settling down at the table, the dowager asked, "Now, what are we to do with her? Death by poisoning would suit me."

Knowing the dowager's secret predilection for Penny Dreadful novels, Evie smiled. "I doubt we'll have to resort to such extreme measures." Sighing, Evie added, "I don't remember life in the country ever being so complicated." When Evie had first settled into Halton House, she had been quick to fall in love with it all. A season for everything and ever so many activities to try to fit in. "What if this is only the beginning and she means to take over everything?"

"That is precisely her intention and that is why we must nip her recalcitrant attitude in the bud," the dowager said. "Now… Are you going to offer me some tea?"

"Yes, of course. Have some cake too."

"Oh, thank you. Yes, I suppose if we are to do battle with the likes of her, we should keep up our strength," the dowager remarked. "Don't you agree, Edgar?"

"I do, my lady."

Turning back to Evie, the dowager asked, "So, what is the plan? I assume you have a trump card up your sleeve."

Yes, she had. And she'd just used it up.

4

High hopes for a bright new day

Evie had never been happier to wake up to a new day. Since she had made a mess of the previous one, she decided to steer clear of the Hunt Ball debacle and devote her morning to visiting the local tenants.

"Any sign of Tom?" Evie asked.

"No, milady. In your place, I would worry about him driving around in that expensive motor car. What if he never returns?"

Evie chortled. "What do you think he'll do? Sell the car and live out his days in the Riviera?"

"He might."

"It's a Duesenbert and I'm sure it's the first one to be brought into the country. The police would have no trouble tracing it. I think I would give him more credit than to try something so foolish."

"So, you have thought about it," Caro mused.

"No, I'm only humoring you because you are once again talking to me. I hope that means you have forgiven me."

"Not really, milady. I can't help having strong opinions on the matter." Caro lowered her voice to a whisper. "He is only seven years old."

"Will my hats continue to suffer for my sins?"

"I shall try to control my urges, milady."

Reluctantly, Evie turned her thoughts to the previous day. She wished she hadn't tried to intervene by inviting Mrs. Howard-Smith to tea. What had Mrs. Howard-Smith been thinking behaving as she had? It would make their next encounter that much more difficult. People were bound to talk. In fact, Evie suspected Mrs. Howard-Smith would make sure of it.

"Caro, tell cook I will have breakfast in bed. There's no point in setting up the breakfast table just for me. I will be making another attempt to call on the tenants so I will want something hardy to keep me going, please. She knows what I like."

"Very well, milady." Caro opened the bedroom door just as someone knocked on it.

Edgar strode in. "Begging your pardon, my lady. There is someone at the door requesting assistance."

"What sort of help do they need, Edgar?"

"I believe their motor car has broken down not far from here," Edgar explained.

"Use your judgment, Edgar. If you think they look safe, invite them in and ask someone to tend to the car."

"It's a woman, my lady. She looks harmless

enough."

What could she have been doing out on the road at such an early hour and obviously alone? "Caro. I've changed my mind. I will be going down for breakfast. Edgar, please show the lady through to the library."

***

The young woman introduced herself as Miss Phillipa Brady.

Evie recognized her from Mrs. Baker's Delights. She had been the bright young thing who had caught everyone's attention.

"It's very kind of you to offer me shelter, Lady Woodridge." She tilted her head and added, "I think I recognize you from the tea room."

"Yes. Are you passing through?" Evie asked.

"Is that what everyone wanted to know yesterday?"

Evie smiled. "Yes, indeed. You caused quite a stir. But in a good way. I must say, I do love your trousers. They look quite comfortable." The 'bright young things' everyone had been talking about had been making quite a splash with their outrageous ways. Being over thirty years old, Evie felt somewhat left out and a little envious...

"Thank you. They are extremely comfortable. A friend designs them."

"Well. You're just in time for breakfast." Evie showed her through to the morning dining room where they helped themselves to a hearty breakfast of bacon, eggs and sausages as well as Evie's favorite biscuits.

Miss Phillipa Brady did not shy away from all the food on offer and ate with great gusto.

"I couldn't help noticing your accent," Evie remarked.

Phillipa nodded. "Australian. Yes, I'm a long way from home. And, considering I hail from the bush, that's really a long way."

"The bush?"

"Oh, that's what we call the outback… the countryside. My folks run a cattle station. It's what you'd refer to as a ranch."

"And what brings you out this way?"

Phillipa shrugged. "Life. Excitement. The need to seek like-minded people. News from abroad reaches our shores at a snail's pace. I wanted to be at the center of it all. As you can imagine, it's difficult being artistic and adventurous when you're living out in the middle of nowhere. I'm what you might call a bohemian at heart."

Evie laughed. "I believe the correct term nowadays is bright young thing or flapper."

"I don't mind either one," Phillipa said. "In fact, flapper rather suits me. I have been flapping about. There's so much to see and do here."

"Here? In Berkshire?"

"Well, not exactly. I mean in London."

"So, if all the excitement is back in London,

what brings you out this way?"

"A car rally. I will be joining a group I met in London and we'll be driving around. I believe they are also planning a sort of treasure hunt."

"Oh, that does sound rather exciting." Evie wondered if anyone could join. It would be just the thing to break up the routine she knew she would eventually fall into.

Edgar had a brief exchange with a footman and then cleared his throat to announce, "The Dowager Countess of Woodridge."

Which one? And… At this time of morning?

Henrietta entered, her stride determined. "I came as soon as I heard." Noticing the other person sitting at the table, Henrietta acknowledged her with a nod.

Evie made the introductions and explained Phillipa's presence. "Would you like to join us for breakfast?"

Sounding out of breath, the dowager said, "I should eat something, yes. I left the house in rather a hurry. In fact, I left as soon as news reached me."

"How did you get here?" Evie asked.

"Hobson drove me, of course."

Her chauffeur had driven her and yet she looked and sounded out of breath.

Holding her hand to her chest, Henrietta said, "I have notified Sara. I appeared to have been first in with the news. She knew nothing about it. She still has her breakfast in bed and her maid has always been rather slow and unusually disinterested in news."

Evie spread some strawberry jam on her toast. "I am almost anxious to hear the news, but I imagine you will tell me in good time."

Across the table, Phillipa stifled a laugh.

"She's dead," Henrietta declared.

The knife slipped out of her hold. Evie realized this would happen in instalments… for greater effect, she thought.

"Found early this morning. Everyone is in shock. Personally, I don't mind admitting I have been entertaining mixed feelings. While I never wished her ill, this does rather work in our favor."

Evie straightened. "Grandmama, you are beginning to scare me. Who died?"

"Oh, did I not mention it? Mrs. Howard-Smith."

5
Mrs. Howard-Smith… Dead?

"According to my butler who heard it from a reliable source, Dr. Browning received a telephone call in the middle of the night, after which he sped his way through the village, heading toward Witford Hall, that's Mrs. Howard-Smith's home, to attend to Mrs. Howard-Smith." The dowager took a quick sip of tea and then resumed telling her tale. "I'd had a restless night and thought I heard several vehicles drive by, but I didn't bother getting up, although I did consider ringing for my maid. After some thought, I decided I really didn't have the heart to wake her up."

Evie cusped her hands around her teacup. "So, your news hasn't actually been confirmed."

"Oh, but it has. Do you think I would come to you with unverified news? It would be dreadfully unkind of me to unsettle you for no good reason." The dowager lifted her chin. "I'm almost offended that it would even occur to you."

"My apologies, Henrietta. How thoughtless of

me." Evie glanced at Phillipa and noticed the news hadn't affected her appetite. "So, how exactly did you confirm it?"

"Oh, I called Barton and Brown. They took her away early this morning."

Barton and Brown... The funeral directors.

"They've taken care of us for too many years to begrudge me the information."

Evie picked up her fork only to set it down again. She had well and truly lost her appetite.

Mrs. Howard-Smith.

Dead.

"I didn't detect any signs of illness yesterday. Do you think she might have had a condition of sorts?"

"I can only imagine her temperament might have had something to do with her demise," the dowager said. "You can't go through life being disagreeable and not pay the price. I'm sure the French have a saying for it. They seem to do so for so many things." The dowager struck a pensive pose. "*Mauvais sange* comes to mind. They believe unnecessary worrying turns your blood bad, resulting in illness. They must have some special fate for those wicked souls who make others' lives miserable."

Evie mused, "I had a French nanny who would often accuse me of turning her blood bad. I never understood what she meant. She had a nervous disposition and would twitch whenever she saw me skipping about or, heaven help her...

or me, running. She used to warn me against it all. Nothing pleased her more than when I slept."

The dowager shrugged. "I suppose we shall have to swallow our pride and attend the funeral. I will, of course, dress in full mourning on the day out of respect for the family." The dowager turned to Phillipa. "You say you are only here for a brief time?"

Phillipa nodded. "Only until my motor car can be fixed."

The dowager turned her attention to her breakfast. "Oh, scones for breakfast. That's a novelty. But then, I forget. You don't call them scones." Leaning in, she whispered to Phillipa, "We are still getting used to Evangeline's ways. I'm afraid I still have a long way to go before I embrace the idea of biscuits for breakfast."

"I asked cook to prepare a hearty meal," Evie explained. "She knows how much I enjoy my biscuits. Although, to be fair to me, I do call them scones now."

A footman strode in carrying a fresh pot of tea and some coffee.

When Edgar cleared his throat, Evie curved her eyebrows. Another visitor?

"Mr. Winchester."

"Oh," the dowager exclaimed with interest. "My early visit is paying dividends. When I got up this morning, I did not dream I would be meeting the elusive Mr. Winchester."

"There's nothing elusive about him,

Henrietta. But this is a surprise." Evie turned slightly and watched Tom enter the dining room.

He wore one of his country suits in a pale shade of brown and a pristine white shirt. His tie had been so expertly arranged, she'd almost believe he'd had assistance from a valet.

He looked surprised to find Evie had company. For a split second, Evie thought he also looked reluctant to step into a room with three women in it. Standing still, his gaze jumped from one to the other. Evie almost expected him to make a hasty retreat.

"I see you took me up on my offer to visit Berkshire," Evie said and hoped he would read that as his cue.

"Yes, I arrived yesterday but I didn't wish to bother you so late so I stayed in the village."

The explanation suited their purposes of establishing a story for Mr. Winchester who also happened to be Tom, her chauffeur…

If he thought he could explain his disappearance with nothing but a blithe remark, he had another think coming. But what had brought him here so early? "Do join us for breakfast." Evie turned toward Edgar who'd already jumped into action preparing another place setting at the table.

After they had left the Duke of Hetherington's house several weeks before, they had returned to London and Tom had resumed his chauffeuring duties without any sense of awkwardness or reference to his role playing. Now, he appeared to have stepped back into his alter ego. Why?

She wished he had telephoned before coming. The circumstances at Halton House would call for delicate handling. At the moment, they only had to worry about Henrietta. But the dowagers were bound to drop in at any time together and, eventually, their curiosity would prompt them to dig deeper…

Since they would be sticking to their story and claiming to be childhood friends, the inevitable questions were bound to be asked. Why had Evie never mentioned him before? In fact, Sara had already asked her that very question. Of course, she could easily dismiss it by saying she had many friends she never mentioned.

However, they would need to navigate this particular ocean with care. Both Henrietta and Sara had met her mother and grandmother when they had traveled to England for Evie's wedding. Evie knew they corresponded. One stray remark would be enough to end Tom's undercover ruse.

Introducing him to Henrietta and Phillipa, Evie tried to keep her tone casual when she said, "Tom has been touring the country. In fact, I recently spent a few days at Yarborough Manor in Yorkshire and he dropped in for a visit." Before anyone could comment, Evie changed the subject. "The dowager has just come by to deliver some sad news. A local died during the night."

"Yes, I heard a rumor in the village," Tom said as he strode toward the buffet table and helped himself to breakfast. "Did you know her?"

"I met her a couple of days ago and… she had tea with me yesterday," Evie said as she tried to gage her butler's response to Tom's presence.

Both he and Caro knew her chauffeur, Tom Winchester, had been parading around as Mr. Tom Winchester. Belatedly, Evie wondered if they should have chosen another name for his alter ego. Regardless, Edgar gazed into space, his look as disinterested as ever. Evie knew Tom must have had a word with him, coming to some sort of understanding with him. It seemed to be working for him, so she decided to leave it alone.

Tom settled down next to her at the table. "Where did you first meet her?"

"At Mrs. Baker's Delights. It's a local village tea room."

"She had been conspiring against us," Henrietta declared.

"Long story," Evie mouthed.

"I'd love to hear it," Tom murmured right back.

"Evangeline," Henrietta said. "Sara and I have been thinking of throwing a dinner party to welcome you back. Of course, Mrs. Howard-Smith's unfortunate demise has rather thrown a dampener on our plans. If I believed in the afterlife, I would have no trouble imagining Mrs. Howard-Smith having a jolly good laugh at our expense."

"What do you believe in?" Phillipa asked.

Henrietta made a dismissive hand gesture. "Well, we must transform into something but I doubt it is into a mirror image of ourselves. Perhaps we become butterflies. I suppose I do believe in some sort of existence. I just haven't really given it much thought."

"Hindus believe in reincarnation," Phillipa remarked.

"Oh, and there are quite a few of them," Henrietta said with interest. "With so many people believing in reincarnation, I will have to give it some serious thought."

"I think much depends on how well you've behaved yourself in this life," Phillipa offered.

Henrietta's eyes widened slightly.

"They call it karma," Phillipa added. "If you've been bad, you might come back as a mangy dog or a beggar."

"There's always a catch." Shaking her head, Henrietta finished her tea. "Well, I must get on with my day. And then I'll need to rest because I should like to look my best for the service. I always fear being so close to one's final resting place might tempt the grim reaper into speeding things along." Henrietta sighed. "I dare say this will change everything."

"How so?" Evie asked.

"Well, now that she is gone, the mutineers are without their leader. The Vicar's wife might have appeared to lead the breakaway group, but I believe the true instigator remained in the background. I don't wish to speak ill of the dead. Yes, I mean Mrs. Howard-Smith. In any case, we should be humble in our victory. Perhaps we should offer the use of Halton House. I think that should appease everyone. I can't imagine the Countess will want to hold the ball at her house. They will be in full mourning."

"It sounds like you have your hands full," Phillipa said as she pushed back her chair. "I suppose I should see if my motor car has been fixed. If you could point me in the right direction…"

"We'll come out with you," Evie offered.

The dowager stopped at the door. "Am I expected for dinner tonight?"

Evie hadn't given it any thought. Now that the dowagers had moved out, she would have to start issuing invitations. "Henrietta. This is your home. You don't need to wait for an invitation."

"Is that a yes or a no?"

Evie tried to remember if she had tackled the issue of Henrietta and Sara moving out. No… They had been diverted. "Yes, you are expected tonight. This is your home," she insisted. Evie exchanged a glance with Edgar and knew that would be enough to set the wheels in motion for the evening meal which she might otherwise have eaten on a tray.

They strode out into a fine day full of spring

sunshine. Evie took a discreet peek at her watch to see if she would still manage to trek out as planned to meet the tenants. Looking up, she caught sight of a vehicle parked several feet away from the entrance.

A bright red roadster…

Mr. Winchester's vehicle of choice.

Evie wondered where he had procured this one.

"We must talk," Tom whispered.

Waving to the dowager, Evie replied in a hushed tone, "In a minute."

When the dowager's car disappeared down the driveway, Evie guided them around the house. "Phillipa's car broke down. I'm hoping Edmonds will be able to fix it." The stable hand had learned all he could from her late husband's chauffeur who had retired a couple of years before. "If that fails, we should be able to get some help in from the village. And, now that I think about it, I am without a chauffeur." Evie glanced at Tom. "Perhaps Edmonds will consider a promotion."

"There's no real need for that. If you require a chauffeur, I will be more than happy to drive you around."

"Oh, how kind of you to offer. And, I suppose you have your own car." She tilted her head and smiled at him. "Do you?"

"You know very well I do."

Lowering her voice, she asked, "And are you

about to tell me how you came by this particular car?" If she thought about it, the story he had given her the last time should have sounded far-fetched. Yet, she had fallen for it.

"Where there are means, there are ways."

Frowning, she tried to understand what he meant. Once again, she thought about the story he had fabricated for himself. A self-made millionaire. An oil man who'd struck it rich in the oil fields of Oklahoma. According to his tale, Mr. Winchester had a vast fortune to dip into.

"Let's leave it at that," he said.

"For now," Evie agreed. "However, at some point, I might wish to push for more information. Otherwise, I fear I might come across as being too naïve."

They found Edmonds under the motor car whistling a happy tune. Tom crouched down and made his presence known. A moment later, Edmonds slid out from under the motor car and promptly jumped to his feet.

"I'm afraid it's not good news, milady. The water pump is leaking. I could try to fix it but I can't guarantee it will last."

"So, what do you suggest we do?" Evie would be as hospitable as possible, however, Phillipa would still need to have her vehicle up and running.

"I'll have a talk with the local repairman. He might have a spare part but I doubt it."

Phillipa brushed her hands across her face.

"Well, I'm in a bit of a pickle."

Evie gave her a reassuring smile. "You can stay here for as long as you need to. When do you have to meet your friends?"

"In about a week. I suppose that should be enough time to fix the car."

"Would you like to let them know? You can use the telephone to contact them, but first, you might want to get settled in. I'll ask the housekeeper to organize a room for you."

Evie strode back inside with Phillipa and left her in Mrs. Arnold's capable hands.

Back outside, she hurried her step and found Tom making his way toward her. "Finally," she said.

"Let's walk and talk," he suggested.

"Where did you disappear to yesterday? Caro's imagination has been running wild."

"Since you're going to stay here for a while, I wanted to get the lay of the land and find out who's who," he explained.

Before Evie had set off on her return trip from America to England, her grandmother had organized for Tom to become her chauffeur. Recently, Evie had discovered her grandmother had actually hired someone with a very special set of skills.

To start with, Tom had been able to transform himself from her chauffeur to a well-dressed and well-spoken gentleman. He had also displayed an uncanny ability to fabricate a credible background story for himself.

"Questions are being asked about Mrs. Howard-Smith's death," he said.

Evie missed a step. Grabbing hold of his arm, she managed to steady herself. "Are you about to tell me she died under suspicious circumstances?" Evie buried her hands inside her pockets. When her fingers collided with a piece of paper, she remembered the telegram she had received the previous day.

Now would not be a good time to bring up the subject and share the news. No doubt, the letter would find its way to another pocket, which meant she could once again delay making the decision…

"Yes. It appears she died of suspicious circumstances."

Or maybe now would be as good a time as any since the news only kept getting worse…

6

Suspicious circumstances? Please explain

"How did you come by that information?" Evie asked, her voice lowered to a whisper. Not that anyone would be able to hear them. They were now on a path leading to the folly and well out of anyone's hearing or even sight.

"I am staying at the pub. It's quite the center of information. By the way, do you own the pub?"

"The Woodridge Arms?" Evie shook her head. "The current owners are tenants. Some pubs are named after local landowners or coat of arms. If memory serves, one of the first Earl's relatives established it but it has since changed hands."

"Anyhow," Tom continued. "when I went down to breakfast, everyone appeared to be talking about the unexpected death."

Evie pressed her hands against her cheeks. It all seemed surreal. "So, tell me about this rumor you've heard."

"One of the maids at the pub knows a housemaid who happened to be attending to Mrs. Howard-Smith during the night when she became ill."

"Did she give any details?"

"The maid said Mrs. Howard-Smith had been physically sick. Before that, she'd complained of nausea."

Evie didn't like the sound of that. "Did she happen to mention when Mrs. Howard-Smith began complaining of feeling ill?" She hoped it hadn't been soon after having tea with her.

Tom stopped and looked at Evie. "Not that I know of. Is that something you are particularly interested in?"

"The woman had afternoon tea at my house," Evie admitted. "So, yes. I am interested." She brushed a hand across her face. "When the dowager broke the news to me this morning, I asked if she had suffered from a condition. It seemed natural to want to know. If I asked that question, so will others." Tilting her head, she gave him a brisk and somewhat self-mocking smile. "Do you know what else I imagine people will ask once they find out Mrs. Howard-Smith had tea at my house?"

"If there had been any animosity between you and if you had reason to kill her?"

Evie looked surprised. "Well, you were quick to jump to conclusions."

He produced a chuckle. "Countess

Woodridge, did you or did you not wish Mrs. Howard-Smith ill?"

"Heavens, that is no joking matter. How did we get onto the subject?"

"I think we put two and two together. People are bound to entertain a few assumptions. If Mrs. Howard-Smith had complained of feeling nauseous then, it stands to reason, they will assume she became ill from something she ate or something she drank. What did you have for afternoon tea? Or, more to the point, what did you feed her?"

Instead of answering, Evie asked, "Do you think the police will become involved?" And, if they did, would they question her? She could not be the first Woodridge to shroud the family name with shame and scandal. "Would it be premature of me to wish I had never returned to England?"

"A part of me wishes to assure you there is nothing to worry about, but my job is to prevent any harm from coming to you and to try to foresee any circumstance before they become an issue."

"Yes… about that. We never really discussed your extra duties. Is that why you chose to go incognito as soon as we arrived?"

"My job is to do everything I can to keep you safe," he repeated.

Feeling overwhelmed by the morning's news, Evie wished to change the subject, at least long enough to clear her head.

Evie could come up with a way to distract herself. She knew she could. However, it seemed inappropriate to comment about the lovely weather they were enjoying. So, she settled for talking about her own well-being, which to some might seem rather insensitive… "Is there a particular reason why my grandmother took such precautions?" She'd never asked. For all she knew, the family might have received a threat or some sort of trigger to prompt them into taking precautions.

"I believe your grandmother heard about an incident with an heiress on the West Coast and she decided she didn't wish to spend her final years worrying."

Why worry when you could hire someone to worry on your behalf, Evie thought. Swinging around, she said, "I believe I am in a state of shock over Mrs. Howard-Smith." She took a few steps, giving herself some space and came to a stop when she reached an oak tree.

How could they find out more detailed information?

It would surely be too soon to pay the family a visit and offer her condolences.

"Lemon cake," Evie finally said. "That's what we had for tea." Evie closed her eyes and tried to remember if Mrs. Howard-Smith had eaten any cake.

"Individual cakes or one cake?"

"We both had a portion from the same cake.

At least, I think she did," Evie answered. "If there had been something in the cake, I would have been affected too." She turned and frowned. "Is that where our minds are going?"

Tom slipped his hands inside his pockets. "Something made her sick. It could have been something she ate."

"In that case, we'll want to know if she ate dinner." How reliable would the maid at the pub be? Could Tom ask her to do some prodding?

"What prompted you to come this morning?" Evie asked. "After all, people die all the time and a suspicious death wouldn't necessarily put me in danger."

Tom looked into the distance. "I heard another rumor."

"Welcome to life in a small village." Evie pushed out a breath. "What else are people talking about?"

"Everyone knows Mrs. Howard-Smith had tea with you. Apparently, someone overheard her say she had to hurry off because you were expecting her."

Tapping her chin, Evie mused, "The committee meeting. She mentioned attending one before coming to Halton House. I assume they held it at Mrs. Baker's Delights."

"According to the rumors flying about," Tom continued, "someone warned her to take care. Why do you think they did that?"

Evie tried not to laugh but the situation

sounded too absurd. "There's a feud of sorts going on." She put both hands up. "While I somehow became caught up in the middle of it all, I have nothing to do with it. In fact, I tried to reason with the woman."

"If the police decide to look into her death, they will probably try to retrace her steps. That means they will want to speak with you."

"I hope it doesn't come down to that." It really wouldn't do for the Countess of Woodridge to be held under suspicion. "By the way, do you have a middle name?"

"Why do you ask?"

"I feel we should play it safe. The dowagers haven't met my chauffeur yet. I think having a different name will lessen the risk of discovery."

Tom looked down at the ground and appeared to inspect his shoes. His lips barely moved when he murmured, "I'm plain Tom Winchester."

"We'll have to think of something. How about Royce?" Evie nodded. "Yes, I believe Royce will suit you just fine."

"Do I get a say in the matter?"

"You did, a moment ago."

7

Meet and greet

"I'm glad to say I'm finally making some progress. I had never realized we had such a diverse group of tenants."

Evie and Tom strode into the Woodridge Arms and settled at a table. Evie did not fail to notice she'd drawn everyone's attention to her and almost felt compelled to stand on a chair and formally introduce herself. "Are they still staring?"

"You can't blame them for being curious," Tom said.

"I hope they can relax and go about their business. I wouldn't want them to feel awkward just because the lady of the manor has dropped by." In fact, she wanted them to get used to seeing her around the village. When she'd first married, she had known she would have to meet her responsibilities to the county and so she had become involved in as many events as she could manage. Even so, her life had remained quite insulated. She'd certainly never stepped out on her own. Had times changed that much? She didn't think twice about walking to the village by herself now. She couldn't remember ever seeing Sara or Henrietta doing so. Although, she understood they hailed from a different era…

"They must be curious to know what I'll do now. As the Countess, my role had been well-defined. Now… I'm a widow and I feel I must discover what my role is. So… I guess I will have to make it up as I go." At least, until Seth Halton grew up and took over the reins, she thought.

"She's coming," Tom said.

Evie turned slightly and saw a young woman dressed in a neat blouse and coat approaching a table.

After visiting several tenants' farms, Tom had begun to make hints about getting lunch and he had thrown in the extra incentive of talking with the maid from the pub who had been so informative.

"I'll be back shortly." Tom rose and went to have a word with the young woman.

Moments later, he returned to the table and introduced Meg Harrison.

"Thank you for agreeing to speak with us," Evie said.

"As I told Mr. Winchester, I'm afraid I don't have any more information. I only know it all happened unexpectedly and took everyone by surprise."

"So, Mrs. Howard-Smith hadn't been

complaining of an illness before last night," Evie said.

"No, according to my friend, she had been as fit as a fiddle. Always so busy."

Evie asked. "She took an interest in local events?"

"Oh, yes. She liked to be involved. So much so, she spread out to local areas."

Only to tread on other people's toes, Evie thought. "How far is Witford Hall from here?" She thought she had heard Henrietta mention the distance, but she couldn't remember with any certainty.

"It's a fair distance. Close to an hour away unless you drive."

An hour away… It seemed odd that anyone would have agreed to allow Mrs. Howard-Smith to host the ball in the first place.

"If I hear anything new I'll be sure to let Mr. Winchester know. I'm sorry, it's my half day off and I'm meeting someone." Meg Harrison rose from the table. "I'm sorry I couldn't be of any more help, milady."

"Oh, but you were wonderful. Thank you for your time."

Tom walked her back to her table. As he rejoined Evie, another young woman joined Meg Harrison, evidently to have lunch.

Tom sat down and said, "She's going to ask her friend to find out if Mrs. Howard-Smith had dined at her house."

"Meg's friend shouldn't have any trouble getting that information." It would only be a matter of asking a footman. "As you said, if the police find anything suspicious about her death, they are bound to retrace her steps," Evie said. "I suppose I should prepare to be questioned." And have a few ready explanations, she thought. "I only hope this doesn't spin out of control."

"What are you afraid will happen?" Tom asked.

"The committee ladies came across as being somewhat unpredictable. So, I'm not sure. However, I get the feeling I need to keep my guard up." Giving Tom a brisk smile, she asked, "So, what can you recommend for lunch?"

A wave of murmurs swept around the pub.

"Oh, this is thrilling," Evie said. "I believe we are in the midst of a news outbreak. How exactly does this work? Do we sit here waiting for someone to approach us or do we join the others? Look, over there. That group appears to be quite excited. Oh… They are now looking toward us. I think we're about to receive the news."

Tom shook his head. "If I had to guess, I'd say you are the news."

***

"The Orchard. I suppose that means they grow apple trees. I believe we have come full circle," Tom said as he came to a stop outside a farmhouse. "The next farm up the road is Hollyhock."

After lunch, they had resumed their tour, meeting and greeting the local tenants who had all been polite and informative. Not a single one had complained to her, which reflected well on the agent.

Evie looked down the lane toward Hollyhock Farm. While most tenancies were separated by cultivated land, The Orchard appeared to be an extension of Hollyhock farm.

Evie followed Tom who'd already headed toward the gate. The rustling sound of leaves drew her attention to a tree growing on the other side of the high wall. She couldn't tell for sure, but she thought she could see someone looking down at them.

Tom gave the bell by the gate a tug. After a few moments, he shook his head. "I don't think anyone is home."

Turning slightly, Evie slanted her gaze and looked toward the tree. "I think we're being watched," she whispered.

"If you're right, then the tenant doesn't wish to speak with you. What do you want to do?"

"We'll walk around. I didn't get a proper look at the outer buildings. Not that I'd be able to tell if there is anything wrong with them." As they rounded the high stone wall, they came out onto a clearing. Neat rows of trees formed a pretty pattern that stretched down a hill. "That's a lot of apples."

Tom patted the stone wall. "This looks ancient."

"A lot of these buildings have been around for a couple of hundred years." Evie pushed out a breath. "Okay. If you're not going to bring it up, then I guess I will. Who do you think spread the rumor about me inviting Mrs. Howard-Smith to afternoon tea?"

"It's not actually a rumor since you did invite her."

"Yes, but it's not something I advertised to the whole county."

They continued to walk along the outer perimeter, their attention on the landscape.

"If Mrs. Howard-Smith's maid spoke with Meg at the pub then she might have mentioned it to someone else. That's usually how information spreads around."

"I'd like to know how it then became distorted. What possible reason would people have for embellishing the truth? I didn't poison her. And why is everyone now talking about poison? Where did they get that information from?"

Tom smiled. "Actually, I believe you mentioned it too."

Oh, she had…

"Even without knowing all the facts, if the woman had suffered from nausea, it would make sense to think of poison," Evie reasoned. "Still, that doesn't give people the right to point the finger of suspicion at me."

"You're clearly not comfortable being the topic of conversation."

"I suppose I should be amused by it all. People seem to be. At least, that's something. They're not really being malicious about it." Tilting her head in thought, she asked, "Is it possible they might be using me for entertainment?"

"It wouldn't be the first time a high-ranking member of society became…"

As Tom struggled to find the right word, Evie suggested, "A subject of ridicule?"

He gave her a small smile. "Admit it. It is far more interesting to think the Countess of Woodridge set out to solve a problem by poisoning the troublemaker than to think Mrs. Howard-Smith died from an undiagnosed heart condition."

Had the maid overheard the doctor providing the family with his conclusions? "How do these rumors even start?"

8

The main topic of conversation: feathers and pineapples

"Caro, you're fussing with my hair. You normally know exactly what you want to do. What's wrong? You look puzzled." And she'd been murmuring under her breath. Too softly for Evie to make any of it out.

"I'm a little confused, milady, but I should soon get it all sorted out in my head."

"Can I help?" It would be a small gathering of five for dinner but she still needed to look presentable.

"You really shouldn't mind me, milady. I just thought I heard Mr. Edgar say Mr. Winchester would be joining you for dinner tonight."

Evie gave an insouciant shrug. "Oh, I see. Is there a problem with that?"

Caro frowned. "Not exactly, milady. Only… Well, I thought Mr. Winchester had gone on his merry way, so to speak. In fact, I convinced myself we had seen the last of him. Now he's back… I just don't see how it will all work out."

Evie smiled at her. "We have a plan, Caro."

Caro stilled and gave her a furtive glance.

Grinning, Evie said, "If anyone asks, my chauffeur's name is Royce."

Caro's lips pursed. "I see. And what if Royce is required to drive you and Mr. Winchester somewhere?"

Evie's grin widened. "Why would he do that? Mr. Winchester is perfectly capable of driving himself."

Caro rolled her eyes. "I'm glad you can see the funny side of it, but I'm really concerned. Someone should be. Think of your credibility, milady. How can anyone believe what you say when you are fibbing about this?"

"Really, Caro. You are worrying about nothing." Evie picked up a necklace and studied it. After a moment, she asked, "Has Mr. Winchester's presence been talked about downstairs?"

"That's just it, milady. Everyone seems to be quite fine with the whole setup. In fact, I heard Mrs. Arnold mention both Mr. Winchester and the chauffeur in the same breath, referring to them as separate people. Perhaps my imagination is not up to the task."

"Don't be so hard on yourself, Caro. You are wonderfully creative. Just look at what you do with my hats. Creativity is practically the same as being imaginative. I'm sure with a little effort, you will get the hang of it." Evie subjected her dress to a close scrutiny just in case Caro had decided to take her frustration out on it.

"Will Mr. Winchester be staying at the house?"

Evie gave it some thought and realized she couldn't really answer with any certainty because she had no idea what Mr. Winchester had planned. "I think he might wish to remain at the pub, for the time being." Did she even have a say in the matter? Tom hadn't bothered consulting with her. He'd had plenty of opportunities during the long drive from London. Yet, he'd kept the information to himself.

Caro gave a small shake of her head.

"Clearly, you don't approve."

"It's not my place to hold any opinions on the matter, milady. I'm sure you know what's best."

Evie watched Caro as she placed a black beaded headband on her head and focused on getting the row of feathers to sit properly.

When Caro stepped back to admire her handiwork, Evie smiled with approval. Her maid really did have a special touch with mixing and matching.

"Now to face the dowagers." By now, they would have heard the rumors floating around the village. Evie strode to the door and turned to say something only to gasp.

The feathers that had adorned her headband wafted around her.

"Caro. I believe I'm molting."

"I'm ever so sorry, milady. I don't know

what's come over me."

So much for not holding any opinions on the matter, Evie thought.

***

Evie entered the drawing room and found the small gathering in full swing. Tom had dressed appropriately in his tails and white waistcoat and stood next to Phillipa chatting with the ease of old friends.

Earlier, Evie had sent Caro to ask if Phillipa had brought something suitable to wear. If she hadn't, Evie had been quite prepared to lend her a dress. To her surprise, Phillipa traveled light but quite ready for any occasion.

Sara sat next to Henrietta who appeared to be deep in conversation with a gentleman Evie didn't recognize.

"Ah, here is our hostess," Henrietta exclaimed.

"My apologies," Evie offered. "I had a mishap with some feathers."

"Oh, yes… I see. And you're still having trouble with them." Henrietta pointed to a feather wafting down and continued by saying, "I have taken the liberty of inviting Mr. Townsend. You might not have met him. He owns Bradley Park nearby. He took it over after you returned to America."

Oh, yes. Evie remembered hearing the sad

news about his brother dying during the last days of conflict. "It's a pleasure to meet you, Mr. Townsend."

"Likewise, Lady Woodridge and, it's Everett, please. Since hearing of your arrival, I had made a point of paying you a visit sometime in the near future but then Lady Woodridge called on me this afternoon and extended the invitation."

"The more the merrier. You do us a great favor, Everett. Otherwise, it might only have been Mr. Winchester and us ladies."

"Everett's Bradley Park used to be famous for its greenhouse," Henrietta said.

"It's still there, Lady Woodridge. And still flourishing."

"Oh, please call me Henrietta. With so many Lady Woodridges here it might become rather confusing. What was I saying? Oh, yes. Your greenhouse."

Evie nodded. "I remember hearing mention of it. It's famous for something. It will come to me."

"No need to strain yourself, Evangeline. Everett's greenhouse is famous for growing succulent pineapples. I believe his family first introduced them back in the 1800s."

"We were by no means the first to introduce them to England," Everett said.

"No, but you were one of the first we knew of," Henrietta said. "It was quite extravagant. I remember attending my first dinner party and being in awe of the centerpiece which had included a pineapple sourced from Bradley Park."

Everett smiled. "One of my astute ancestors caught onto the lucrative business of renting them out as a table decoration. Nowadays, they are imported. While they are far too costly to grow, we still manage it."

Evie kept her eyes peeled on any shared looks between Henrietta and Sara. So far, neither one had mentioned the rumors flying around.

"Evangeline. The funeral date has been set," Henrietta announced.

So much for avoiding the subject.

"Edward Howard-Smith is devasted by his loss," Henrietta continued. "He was a devoted husband."

"Were there any children?" Evie asked.

"No, thank goodness for that. One must be pragmatic. He shouldn't have any trouble finding a new wife. In fact, I'm sure there'll be quite a few prospective brides lined up at the funeral." Glancing over at Phillipa, the dowager added, "If your guest is still here, she might want to attend the service."

"I get the feeling she's not quite ready to settle down yet," Evie said. At a signal from Edgar, she invited everyone to proceed through to the dining room.

"Of course, you needn't bother to present yourself as a candidate," Henrietta observed. "I believe the family is quite stringent when it comes to scandal. They will not abide it. And it might be some time before you can shake off the stigma of being labeled a poisoner."

As Sara strode on ahead, she murmured, "I thought you were not going to bring that up, mama."

"But everyone is talking about it," Henrietta defended. "It seems silly to avoid the subject."

"I'm sure I don't know what you are talking about." Evie took her place at the table and turned her attention to the centerpiece display, giving Edgar a nod of approval.

"The doctor has met with the family and he has given them the unfortunate news. Mrs. Howard-Smith died of a heart attack but there are suspicious circumstances as suggested by the presence of the police at Witford Hall."

Evie exchanged a look with Tom. They certainly hadn't heard about this. "When did this happen?"

"A short while ago. I had been about to set off when I saw Dr. Browning's wife rushing toward the vicarage. I waited several minutes and then I sent my butler over to make inquiries. He returned with the news conveyed to him by the Vicar's maid." Henrietta gave a knowing nod. "Yes, the maid is rather sweet on my butler. In fact, he has several admirers, which bodes well for me as we are kept well-informed by young maids wishing to ingratiate themselves with him."

Evie tried to sort the information out in her mind. The doctor had been at Witford Hall when the police had arrived. He must have then passed on the information to his wife who had rushed off to the vicarage.

Evie took a small sip of wine and went through it all again. Finally, she said, "The police went to inform the family they are treating Mrs. Howard-Smith's death as suspicious but the doctor had thought she had died of natural causes. That doesn't quite make sense."

"Oh, I think you might be right," Henrietta agreed. "Or the information might have been tampered with. However, this does not change the facts. There are suspicious circumstances."

Yes, they had already known that, but the information had been based on unsubstantiated rumors.

Evie took another sip of wine. "And why exactly is the finger of suspicion being pointed at me?"

"Everyone knows you had her over for tea," Henrietta said. "In another era, you might have been accused of witchcraft."

"How comforting." Evie turned her attention to the food arranged on her plate. The conversation switched back to pineapples and she heard Everett Townsend mention something about the Dutch being the first to cultivate it and introduce it to England where it had first appeared at Hampton Court in 1692. Although, the first true crop of British pineapples had been grown in the 1700s in Richmond.

Everett Townsend seemed to be very knowledgeable on the subject. So much so, Evie realized she couldn't stake a claim on any particular subject. She decided to remedy the lapse as soon as she could find a subject worth pursuing.

She concluded her train of thought by wondering how this lack of knowledge reflected on her. Had no one ever encouraged her to take an interest?

Halton House contained a vast library. Evie sat up. There had to be something in there to engage her interest. She would begin her search the next day.

Leaning forward, Evie caught Henrietta's attention. "I still don't quite understand. If the doctor reached one conclusion, how did the police become involved?"

"Perhaps the family is not satisfied with the doctor's diagnosis," Everett suggested. "I believe the Earl of Rosenthal would be influential enough to have the matter looked into."

"Yes, but why wouldn't he accept the conclusion of death by natural causes?" Evie insisted. Surely, it couldn't be a case of living in denial, she thought.

Her eyes landed on Tom who said, "The police must have a solid reason for looking into the death. No amount of influence would sway them to allocate manpower to a lost cause."

Evie looked toward the door. If the police wished to speak with her, they would surely wait until morning…

"When is the funeral?" Evie asked.

"In three days' time," Henrietta said. "I took the liberty of sending a letter of condolence. Also, I propose organizing a somewhat daring expression of our sympathies… extended to the committee ladies."

9

Speculative motives anyone?

Halton House library

"If anyone catches me dangling off the ladder, I will simply say there's method in my madness." Evie had hurried through an early breakfast and had then gone directly to the library where she'd perused the shelves at eyelevel.

Most of the leather-bound tomes within easy reach were about animal husbandry and farming and many had bookmarks sticking out of them suggesting someone had made serious study of them over the years.

Standing on tiptoes, she had perused the next shelves up, which had contained history books with an entire row devoted to the Napoleonic wars. She had sought out the assistance of a footstool to reach the next shelves only to find more history books, mostly focused on kings and queens.

She had then progressed onto the ladder, each rung putting her at eyelevel with a new shelf. As she finished scrutinizing the book spines, she tilted her head from side to side and spied an interesting title… at the far end. By this point, she had climbed up and down the ladder several times.

"Who knew the pursuit of knowledge would require so much physical activity." Thinking she could reach the book from where she stood, she gripped the edge of the ladder and stretched her other hand out as far as she could.

That's when the ladder began tilting.

Evie reacted swiftly by straightening and plastering herself against the ladder. She should have known better than to try to reach the book again. Anyone with common sense would not have tried it again. But… try again she did.

On her second attempt, she managed to grab hold of the book, or perhaps the book grabbed hold of her.

This time, the ladder didn't give her a warning. When she stretched, it followed her.

Her reflexes kicked in and she managed to grab a foothold on the edge of a shelf. When Tom strode into the library, he found Evie trying to balance one foot on the bookcase and the other on the ladder.

"Do you need help?" he asked, his tone casual.

Evie tried to speak through gritted teeth but only managed a growl.

"I'll hold the ladder. Do you think you could try to get back onto it?"

"The book," Evie managed. So close, she thought and decided to release it and get back to safety. However, her finger caught and as she moved back to the ladder, the book slid off and landed with a thud. "Oh, I hope I haven't damaged it."

"I'm sure it's fine," Tom muttered. "My head broke its fall."

Evie looked down and saw Tom clutching his head and then rubbing at a sore spot. "I thought you said you were holding the ladder." She managed to straighten, getting both feet back in place. Taking the greatest care, she climbed down and reached the safety of the floor just as Tom crouched down to pick up the thick volume.

"Introduction to Psychoanalysis by Sigmund Freud. Dare I ask?"

Evie lifted her chin. "I'm taking my mind off… I'm taking an interest."

Tom opened the book and read through the contents. "Freudian slip. That sounds intriguing."

Shifting the ladder, Evie climbed back up and found the spot where the book had been shelved. There were several more like it. She drew one out. A quick look inside the cover page told her it had been published only a couple of years before.

Halton House employed a librarian who came in once a week. She would have to ask him if he had made the purchase. She couldn't remember Nicholas ever showing an interest in the inner workings of the human mind.

Selecting another book, she made her way down. “I think I will start with this one.”

Taking the book from her, Tom flipped through the pages. Stopping, he read, “Taboo and emotional ambivalence.” Taking a step back, he sunk down on a chair and began reading.

“Would you mind finding another book? That’s the one I wish to read.”

Tom signaled to the one that had fallen on his head. “Start with that one. This one has captured my interest.”

“Yes, well… These books are meant to engage my interest, not yours.” Nevertheless, she settled down with the other book.

Half an hour later, Tom said, “Interesting. He talks about neurotics feeling ambivalent about most people in their lives. It’s not something they admit consciously to themselves. While they might love their mother, there are things about her they hate.” He closed the book and stared at Evie. “What are you feeling ambivalent about?”

“No one. Nothing,” Evie answered far too quickly and then admitted she loved everyone she met but she had developed a severe dislike of gossip mongers.

Taking the book from Tom, she scanned through the list of contents and asked, “How did you get on with Phillipa last night?”

Smiling, he said, “She reminded me of a horse, champing at the bit, eager for something to happen.” Leaning back on his chair, he crossed his arms and remarked. "You were slightly on edge last night."

She had tried her best to hide it. "I get the feeling there are people gunning for me. I also believe I haven't given them any reason to dislike me. Not yet." She shifted her gaze to the window and rested her eyes on the scenery. When she had first come to live at Halton House, she had been too involved in her marriage to really appreciate her surroundings. Without realizing it, the peacefulness had been her saving grace, keeping her well-grounded. "I should feel only too happy to assist the police with their inquiries but I do hope I won't have to defend myself."

"If the police do come to question you, think of it as an opportunity to get information." He glanced at the book Evie held. "So, is there something behind this sudden interest in the subject of psychoanalysis?"

The door to the library opened and Edgar announced, "Detective Inspector O'Neill."

Tom's eyebrow curved up. "They sent the big guns."

"Lady Woodridge." The inspector strode up to her, his hand extended. "Thank you for agreeing to see me."

Evie couldn't remember being given the choice. She introduced Tom and gestured toward a group of chairs by the window. The detective wore a spiffy suit suggesting he hailed from the city rather than the nearby town of Reading. "How can I help you, Detective?"

"I trust you have heard the news about Mrs. Howard-Smith."

There had been far too much talk about it for Evie to even attempt to convey an impression of vagueness. Evie gave a nod of acknowledgement. "We have also become aware of the police becoming involved." No pleading ignorance from here on out, Evie thought.

"Yes," the detective mused, "Mrs. Howard-Smith's family asked for a second opinion." The detective drew out a small pocket book and took his time searching for the right page. "It is our understanding Mrs. Howard-Smith met with you recently."

Evie explained she had met the woman for the first time in the village and had then had afternoon tea with her.

"So, you formed an instant friendship."

"I wouldn't go so far as to say that," Evie remarked.

"Then, may I ask why you invited her to tea?"

Evie tried to keep her gaze on the detective but it became a struggle. When she lost the battle, she shifted slightly in her chair and looked at Tom just as he set his mouth into a firm line and gave a small shake of his head.

"I wanted to discuss something with her."

The detective asked, "The Hunt Ball?"

"Yes." How had he found out? Had the

renegade committee sold her out?

"Several people have mentioned you were not happy about the new arrangements," he said.

"I wouldn't exactly say that. Although, after I became aware of a few details I did think it odd that a group of women should abscond with a ball which had been established by the Woodridge family. I wanted to try and reason with Mrs. Howard-Smith."

Surprise registered in the detective's eyes.

Tom gave another slight shake of his head as if to suggest she'd said too much.

"Do you garden, Lady Woodridge?"

"No, not really." Evie's gaze drifted to the garden beyond the window. Since seeing the beautiful blooms at Hollyhock Farm, she had subconsciously been thinking about it… "I've been meaning to take up an interest. So, I suppose I've been thinking about it. Why do you ask?"

Instead of answering, he asked, "How long did Mrs. Howard-Smith stay?"

"Not very long. She became agitated and cut the afternoon tea short."

Tom gave another shake of his head, which Evie ignored.

"Mrs. Howard-Smith took exception to something I said," she continued. "Don't ask me what because I still don't quite know myself. She left in a huff. The next morning, I learned of her demise. And, before you ask, she didn't show any signs of illness. In fact, she'd looked fighting fit. In every sense."

"Did she give any indication of where she might have been headed next?"

"None. Why would she tell me? She only said she had been running late because her committee meeting had run overtime."

Tapping his notebook, the detective persevered, "Did you happen to see in which direction she headed?"

"No, I… I didn't show her out. In fact, it took me a few minutes to recover from the encounter. Her manner had been unjustifiably brusque."

The detective turned toward Tom. "Mr. Winchester is it?"

Tom nodded.

"Can you account for your whereabouts during the last forty-eight hours?"

When Tom finished supplying the information, Evie realized he'd left out a pertinent detail.

The detective looked at his notes. "When exactly did you arrive at Halton?"

"Late in the evening. You can check with the local pub."

Turning to Evie, the detective smiled. "I don't seem to have your time of arrival."

"At about the same time as Mr. Winchester. I can't say for sure, I was rather tired and went straight to bed."

"You have a guest staying with you," the

detective said.

How had that piece of news reached him? “Yes. Miss Phillipa Brady. Her car broke down near here.”

“I would like to speak with her, please.”

How had the detective found out about Phillipa? More importantly, should she be worried about her? Evie only knew what Phillipa had chosen to tell them. What if they had been harboring a criminal?

10

If you can't say anything nice, then don't say anything at all…

"Someone killed her and they're trying to pin it on me."

"You brought me out here to tell me that?" Tom asked.

Evie swung around. "Trees don't tell tales." A sheep bleated in the distance. "Who knows what that sheep is saying, but I'm sure she's not implying I poisoned my guest."

"Out of curiosity, what made you say poison?"

"When did I mention poison?" She gave a shake of her head. "Never mind. These last couple of days have become a haze. In any case, isn't poison a woman's weapon of choice?" Evie shrugged. "I think I read that somewhere or maybe I heard Henrietta say it. She loves reading mysteries." Looking over his shoulder, she said, "The detective is leaving."

"I guess that means Phillipa is in the clear," Tom remarked.

"Why wouldn't she be in the clear?"

Tom shrugged. "What do we really know about her? She appeared from out of nowhere. Somehow, she ended up on your doorstep and she is now a guest at your house. Do you know anyone who can vouch for her?"

A valid point, Evie thought. She hadn't asked about the friends Phillipa planned on joining…

They both stood there on the hill watching the detective getting into his car and driving off. Moments later, Phillipa emerged from the library by way of one of the French doors. After a look around, she spotted them and headed their way.

"It will be interesting to hear her take on the detective's questions." Had he asked Phillipa if she gardened?

"I'm glad to say I'm off the hook," Phillipa called out. When she reached them, she laughed as she said, "Would you believe it… I asked why they had sent a detective all the way from Scotland. I know I can be a bit of a dag, but he asked for it by not explaining Scotland Yard is based in London. How could I have known that?"

Both Evie and Tom tilted their heads.

"Dag?" Evie asked.

"Socially inept," Phillipa explained. "Strange in an odd sort of way. Eccentric. It's actually what we call the lock of wool matted with dung hanging from the hindquarters of sheep. Anyhow, the detective didn't seem to appreciate my sense of humor. He thought I needed to take the matter more seriously. Although, he didn't exactly lead by example when he asked if I gardened."

Evie clicked her fingers. "That must be a clue of sorts." Turning, she walked around in a small circle. "He didn't ask any specific questions about gardening. What's so special about it?"

"Gardeners know about plants," Phillipa suggested.

Evie clicked her fingers again. "Tom and I recently came across a case of a young girl suffering from a rash brought on by exposure to a plant." She looked into the distance. "I think we need to pay Henrietta a visit and ask her about the committee ladies. Let's find out who enjoys gardening."

"I thought you were trying to avoid Lady Woodridge," Tom said.

Evie noticed his lips twitched. Almost as if he wanted to smile. "There's no point in avoiding her. She has already proposed her reckless idea and nothing will stop her from going ahead with it."

An afternoon tea for the committee ladies. With the funeral service only two days away, would Henrietta hold the tea before or after?

"Reckless?" This time, Tom smiled.

"Surely, it's asking for trouble."

"Perhaps Lady Woodridge has a plan," Tom suggested.

"She does. Henrietta wishes to reinstate

herself as the rightful organizer of the Hunt Ball. Are you about to suggest we can use the opportunity to learn something about the ladies attending the tea?"

"Yes. You now know the detective is keen to learn who is interested in gardening."

True.

Tom added, "He is also interested in finding out where Mrs. Howard-Smith went after she stormed out of your house."

She could have visited any number of people but would any of them be willing to admit it?

"What sort of motor car did she have?" Phillipa asked. "I might have seen her out and about. I've been doing quite a bit of driving in the area."

"I have no idea. I suppose I could ask Edgar." Her butler would have noticed.

When they strode back to the house, Phillipa said, "I assume you have a gardener."

Evie had to think hard about it. Of course, they had a gardener, but had she met him? "Oh, it's one of the tenants. He's a bachelor and lives with his brother. I remember the previous gardener retired right before I left. I asked the dowager if she could take care of it and she pretended to be inconvenienced by it all. Secretly, of course, she relished the idea of being at the helm again. I believe she engaged the agent to search for a replacement. She must have written to me about it."

"Do you think we could speak with him?" Phillipa asked.

"Whatever for?" Evie glanced around the estate wondering where he might be found at this time of the day. Too close to midday for him to be out and about, she thought. "We could try the buildings near the stables."

As they changed course, Evie noticed Edgar heading toward them so she slowed down. When he reached her, he said, "There is a letter for Mr. Winchester. It has been forwarded from the London house."

"Thank you. I'll hand it to him." Evie turned to rejoin the others only to stop. "Edgar."

"Yes, my lady."

"Do you remember what Mrs. Howard-Smith's car looked like?"

"I'm afraid not, my lady. I'm not much of a car connoisseur. However, I do recall the color. Green. Forest green."

"Would anyone else have noticed?"

"I shall ask the footman, my lady."

Nodding, she turned only to again stop. "By the way, what is the gardener's name?"

"George Mills, my lady."

Thanking him, Evie hurried to catch up with the others. "There's a letter for you, Tom."

He opened it and drew out another envelope. "It's a telegram. It must have been sent to the London house." He read the message.

Evie tried to read his expression, but his face

gave nothing away.

Instead of sharing the contents, he returned the page to the envelope and tucked it inside his pocket.

"Nothing terribly bad, I hope." Would he tell her if something bad had happened?

"No. Nothing bad."

She didn't push him for more. It would hardly seem fair since she had as yet to share the contents of the telegram she had received. Evie slanted her gaze toward him. What if both telegrams contained the same information?

Phillipa pointed toward the yard. "I see someone with a wheelbarrow. I suppose we could call out ahoy there."

"No need. His name is George Mills."

Phillipa cupped her hands around her mouth and called out his name. "I suppose I should apologize but, as I said, I'm from the bush."

"The bush?" Tom whispered.

"That's the back of beyond," Evie explained. "Did you have a school house nearby?"

Phillipa shook her head. "We would have had to travel two days to reach the nearest one. So, we had a governess." Huffing out a breath, she added, "She practiced strict discipline for two hours at a time with breaks in-between where she let us loose and encouraged us to have fun. I will never have to wonder why I grew up so confused."

Having heard his name called out, George

Mills pulled off his cap and greeted them.

"George. We've been admiring your handy work. Well done. The gardens look absolutely splendid."

"Thank you, milady."

"We were wondering if you could help us out. Are there any plants that might be dangerous? My knowledge of plants is very limited."

"There are plenty of poisonous plants, milady. But none that are grown at Halton House. Although, at some point, there must have been foxglove grown here. There is a framed notice in the gardener's tool shed forbidding the cultivation of foxgloves."

"Why is that?"

"I'm told her ladyship lost a pup to it."

"Which ladyship?"

"Lady Woodridge, milady."

Evie smiled. "Lady Sara or Lady Henrietta?"

George Mills nodded. "Lady Henrietta, milady."

"Does anyone in the district grow it?"

"I'm not sure. All I know is that no one on the estate can grow it. Hollyhock Farm used to grow early bloomers and they won many prizes at the flower show."

"So, apart from killing Lady Woodridge's dog, why exactly is it forbidden?"

"It can be fatal, milady. Not only to livestock but to people too."

11

People can lose their lives in libraries.
They ought to be warned – Saul Bellow

Library, Halton House

"A Manual of Poisonous Plants published in 1910." Evie handed the book to Tom and came down from the ladder just as the mantle clock struck the hour. "We still have some time before we have to head off to Henrietta's afternoon tea. And, if I happen to forget, I hope no one reminds me. This is one afternoon tea I do not look forward to attending." She rang the bell. When the footman appeared, she asked for coffee. "Lots of it, please."

"I had no idea there were so many poisonous plants," Tom said as he skimmed through the pages. "But, so far, I can't find anything on foxgloves."

"I'll keep looking. There's bound to be more books on the subject," Phillipa suggested. "I'm actually surprised your librarian doesn't have some sort of filing system. Oh, I spoke too soon." Phillipa pointed at a set of drawers. "These are catalogue cards." She drew one out. "They indicate the general location of the book by shelf number. I suppose that's better than nothing and there appears to be some cross referencing here."

"You sound knowledgeable," Evie said.

"I have a spinster aunt who enjoys collecting books on every subject under the sun and can talk about nothing else. She has so many books, she employed a librarian to sort them out. She ended up inspiring my aunt to purchase more books and build more bookshelves. In less than a year, she filled them all."

"There's nothing here about foxgloves," Tom declared even as he continued turning the pages.

"Perhaps I should have a look." Evie leaned over his shoulder.

"I spoke too soon. Found something but it's not much," Tom said. "Digitalis Purpurea. Its common name is the Purple Foxglove. It is poisonous to man and livestock, especially horses. It contains the glucosides digitalin, which dilates the pupil."

"What does that mean?"

"Nothing good, I'm sure." He returned to the first chapter. "This is interesting. The use of poisons for criminal purposes, although not nearly so extensive at the present time as during the Middle Ages, still plays an important part in criminal law. In 1906, nearly two thousand people died from poisons."

Evie shivered. "Golly. I feel I should hire a food taster. Then again, I don't think I have it in me to place someone in danger just to save my own neck."

Tom continued reading, "Poisoning of livestock is generally accidental. Large losses occur annually in this way." He closed the book. "I guess Henrietta's dog must have indulged in the wrong plant."

Evie sighed. "Thank goodness they no longer grow foxglove here. I'd hate to think my puppy could have been in danger."

"The puppy you have yet to find?" Tom asked. "Have you actually done something about it?"

"Not yet. But I'm sure the right opportunity will come along soon." She looked up and asked, "Are you having any luck, Phillipa?"

"There are a number of books on plants but, so far, nothing specifically on poisonous plants."

Tom got up to put the book away.

"No, leave it out. I'd like to read it just in case it lists any other plants we should ban from cultivation on the estate."

The edge of Tom's lip kicked up. "In case your puppy accidentally eats it?"

"You can laugh all you like." The footman entered and set down a tray with coffee and cups. "Thank you."

The footman nodded. "I've been asked to convey a message from the cook, Mrs. Horace. She apologizes but there will not be any poppy seed cake for this afternoon's tea. She has prepared a walnut loaf instead, as well as finger sandwiches and the lemon cake you enjoy."

"Oh, that's fine, I'm sure." Although, she couldn't help feeling that might be a lot for only three people.

The footman turned to leave.

"Just a moment. Afternoon tea, did you say?"

"Yes, milady."

"I don't remember organizing it."

"Six to eight guests for tea, milady."

"Thank you." Evie tried to remember when she might have made the arrangement. Striding around the library, she mused, "I have no recollection of inviting anyone to tea."

"That's not a good sign," Phillipa teased. "Are you sure you didn't kill Mrs. Howard-Smith? You might have forgotten."

Coming full circle, Evie stopped in front of the table. "Oh, the coffee. I'll pour. And don't think I didn't notice you both exchanging a look that questioned my focus and possibly suggested I've become absent-minded."

Phillipa laughed and in the next breath, she shouted, "Eureka!"

"I take it you found something of worth?" Evie asked.

Phillipa waved the leather-bound tome. "An account of the Foxglove and Some of Its Medical Uses, published in 1785."

"Fabulous."

Phillipa climbed down from the ladder and

settled at the table to study the contents, saying, "It seems to be both a killer and a savior."

Tom and Evie huddled around her looking over her shoulder as she flipped through the pages. And that's how Lady Woodridge found them when she strode into the library an hour later.

"Here you are," Henrietta exclaimed. "Although, I have no idea what you are doing here. Your guests are waiting."

Evie straightened. "M-my guests? Whatever are you talking about, Henrietta?"

"The committee ladies, of course. Let me remind you. We are humbly extending our hand of friendship and mending fences. I suspect we will be run off our feet. There will be so much to do but it will all be manageable with the extra helping hands." The dowager turned to leave. "Oh, and we should be generous and not mention any of the nonsense that has been going on. This is a time for forgiveness and for forging ahead. Tally-ho."

12

The ship of democracy, which has weathered all storms, may sink through the mutiny of those on board - Grover Cleveland

The drawing room, Halton House

Tom and Phillipa had promised to join Evie for the tea party. Half an hour later and about to drink her second cup of tea, Evie knew they had deceived her. “Duped,” she said against her cup before turning and saying, “Mrs. Hallesberry, would you care for some more tea? It’s my own special blend.” She glanced over at Henrietta who smiled in approval.

When she had expressed her intention to extend the hand of friendship, or some such thing, to the committee ladies, Henrietta had failed to mention the event would be held at Halton House and it would be hosted by Evie.

“Thank you,” Mrs. Hallesberry said.

“Have some cake. It’s made with our own walnuts and the flour comes from one of our tenant farmers,” Evie thought to add even as she held images of wringing Tom’s neck for abandoning her in her hour of need.

Mrs. Hallesberry helped herself to some cake. "There's something about the bereavement process that always manages to stimulate my appetite."

"Mrs. Howard-Smith's leadership will be sorely missed," Mrs. Browning exclaimed as she had been doing for the past half hour. The doctor's wife had produced a handkerchief and had continuously dabbed at the edge of her eyes.

Emotions were definitely running high as well as hot and cold, Evie thought as she noticed the committee ladies casting wary glances at Henrietta.

Had they accepted the invitation out of sheer curiosity or were they prepared to eat humble pie and meet the dowager's demands of full compliance?

The Vicar's wife leaned toward Evie and asked, "Did she seem out of sorts to you, Lady Woodridge? You were the last to see her alive."

Evie wondered at the reason behind Mrs. Ellington's slight exaggeration. "I'm sure others saw her after her visit here. She appeared to be in a hurry to get somewhere else." If some people chose to overstate, Evie decided she retained the prerogative to understate. Mrs. Howard-Smith hadn't just been in a hurry to leave. She'd been desperate. If Evie had been standing in front of her, the woman would have rammed into her, stopping at nothing in order to make her dramatic exit.

Evie remembered the day she'd met her. Mrs. Howard-Smith had been in a hurry to get somewhere else. If the police were trying to trace her movements, they must have reason to believe she had not gone straight home after leaving Halton House. And, if she had visited one of the committee ladies, they would have provided the information to the police.

She looked from one to the other. Yes, they would have told the police everything…

Evie noticed an exchange of glances between Mrs. Hallesberry and the Vicar's wife and decided they knew something but they would not share the information with her.

"I hear she got around quite a bit," Evie said. "I'm sure mine was not the only invitation she accepted on the day."

The furtive glances continued.

Evie looked around to make sure everyone had tea and cake. "In fact, one of my guests thinks she might have seen her about town. What color motor car did she drive?"

"Green with black trimming," Mrs. Penn offered.

Henrietta's spy earned a chastising look from Mrs. Browning. This struck Evie as odd. They were definitely hiding something. They might even be in collusion together… That didn't make any sense to Evie. Any information withheld from the police would only hinder their efforts to get to the truth.

"That could be any number of vehicles in the area," the Vicar's wife exclaimed and set off a wave of agreement from the others.

"Mrs. Howard-Smith had been far too conscientious of her duties to stray from her usual route." Mrs. Browning looked to the others for support and received it with more nods of approval.

Evie bit into a piece of walnut cake. There had to be a reason why they would employ subterfuge. Their deceit would surely do more harm than good. Even if they wanted to… What?

Evie tilted her head in thought. Had Mrs. Howard-Smith had a secret? Were the committee ladies trying to safeguard it?

Evie plunged headlong into thinking about secrets. What would a woman of Mrs. Howard-Smith's standing wish to hide?

Her past?

Henrietta had joked about her family smuggling rum, but what if there was some truth to it? Would it matter that much?

Mrs. Clarissa Penn set her cup of tea down. "We appreciate this conciliatory afternoon tea. It was very gracious of you to extend the invitation, Lady Woodridge."

Henrietta cleared her throat. "In times of loss, one must learn to put one's grievances aside and look forward to a fresh start." She waved her hand. "Bygones."

The remaining members of the mutiny club

were caught off guard. Their eyes widened slightly.

In Evie's opinion, they had two choices. They could either come clean and state their intentions or they could humor Henrietta and play their cards close to their chests.

Personally, Evie would refrain from saying anything that would stir up the still troubled waters.

The Vicar's wife, Mrs. Ellington, expressed a different opinion. "Lady Woodridge, you appear to be under the misguided belief something has changed when, in fact, nothing has changed."

Mrs. Ellington came across as being somewhat combative. Evie would even go so far as to say she had deliberately set out to shock the dowager. While she didn't wish to cast aspersions on the Vicar's wife, Evie found her belligerence out of place.

Henrietta gave the Vicar's wife a warm, sincere smile and employed the utmost politeness to ask, "I'm sorry, are you addressing me or the Countess?"

Evie nearly choked on her tea. Henrietta knew very well Mrs. Ellington had been talking to her.

In order to avoid any further confusion, the Vicar's wife made a point of looking straight at Henrietta. "In honor of our dearly departed friend, we feel it is our duty to forge ahead with the existing plans."

"But how can you possibly think of doing so?"

Henrietta asked. "Witford Hall will be a house in mourning and, therefore, unavailable to host the Hunt Ball."

Glancing around the drawing room, Mrs. Ellington said, "We were hoping to appeal to your better nature."

Henrietta succumbed to a bout of coughing. When she recovered, she said, "You are mistaken if you think you can play that card."

"The Hunt Ball must proceed as planned with all the funds raised going to the local hospital," Mrs. Ellington explained. "Are you prepared to be the one to negate those poor souls the opportunity of reaping the benefit of our charity?"

"Mrs. Ellington, would you care for some tea?" Evie offered.

Henrietta now looked dumbfounded. To her credit, she employed her voice of wisdom tone. "You are referring to the hospital set up by the Woodridge family as well as the ball established by us…"

The Vicar's wife set her cup down, but before she could speak, Mrs. Hallesberry said, "We did not realize you put so much importance on personal gain."

Henrietta spluttered. "Personal gain?"

"Is it any wonder we felt compelled to go our own way," Mrs. Hallesberry continued, her voice rising as if lifted by a wave of emotions. "Someone needed to maintain the integrity of the fundraiser…"

Evie surged to her feet. "Mrs. Hallesberry, I believe enough has been said." Despite her attempt to call for calm, her plea became overshadowed by a torrent of successive accusations from the committee ladies, launched in unison and aimed directly at Henrietta.

It seemed the rebel forces had chosen to bite the hand that fed them.

13

Suspicion always haunts the guilty mind – William Shakespeare

"Nice cake," Tom said as he settled down at the table.

Evie stood by the window and kept her gaze glued on the undulating hills. She had no idea what the Vicar's wife could have been thinking, behaving as she had and toward a woman responsible for her husband's living. Had she always been so antagonistic? Her memory had to be playing tricks on her because Evie could only picture the Vicar's wife as a sweet, generous, even-tempered and softly spoken woman.

Phillipa laughed. "Tom, I think our hostess is giving you the cold shoulder."

"I don't hear her talking to you," Tom said. "In your place, I'd watch out. I have a room at the pub. You, on the other hand, depend on her goodwill."

"I'm thinking," Evie growled softly. "And don't, for a moment, think your absence escaped my notice."

"What did we miss?" Tom asked.

"I witnessed the most unpleasant behavior." Evie shrugged. "I'm not even sure how the kerfuffle started. It's still all sinking in. I thought I would have to call for the doctor to attend to Henrietta. That should give you an indication of what you missed. She has lived through a war and is made of sterner stuff. I've never seen her looking so shocked." Evie swung to face them. "The committee ladies went on the assault and I can't help but think they are hiding something. We need to put our thinking caps on."

"And we need more information," Phillipa said.

Yes, Evie agreed. Unfortunately, they had very little to go on with. "They, more than anyone, would know what Mrs. Howard-Smith did after attending afternoon tea here. Yet, they are not prepared to divulge the information. Why?"

Phillipa helped herself to some tea. "Because they're protecting her."

"Yes, that's what I thought too, but what could someone of her social standing have to hide?"

"An illicit affair."

Phillipa and Evie looked at Tom.

"The second most valuable asset a woman can possess is her reputation," Tom said.

"The second?" Evie had never really thought about it, but if she had to offer her opinion on the matter, a woman's reputation would be uppermost in her mind. "I would have thought it would be at the top of the list."

"A woman's first and foremost valuable asset is her husband."

Phillipa and Evie laughed.

"Think about it," Tom insisted.

"I don't have to," Evie said. "We are talking about a woman of substantial wealth. She didn't need a husband."

Tom held her gaze for longer than he usually did, which made Evie wonder if he had stopped to process the information so he could reach some sort of new conclusion about her.

"Tom might have a point," Phillipa conceded. "Most women do want to marry. If there is money involved, she will most likely look to improve her station in life. She might marry a titled gentleman but those are hard to come by. Also, they come with caveats and usually have expectations of their own. Sometimes, it's not enough to be wealthy."

Oh, yes. Pedigree.

Evie had tackled that particular hurdle when her ability to adjust to a new life had come under close scrutiny. She hadn't just married Nicholas. She had married into a family and a title over three hundred years old.

"So, in order to even get the husband, the woman must have a pristine reputation," Phillipa said. "And the same rule applies if she wishes to keep him."

True.

"Is it possible she might have been having an affair?" Evie asked. And, if so, had someone killed her because of it?

Phillipa expressed the same opinion Evie had just pondered in silence, adding, "Yes, she must have been having an affair. Now to figure out who would hold the strongest objections to an affair and, in turn, the strongest motive to kill."

An affair…

Playing around with the idea, Evie made a mental list of everyone who might be affected. The couple's respective spouses. Their families. Their friends. Any one of them might have decided to take matters into their own hands.

She said, "Her husband loved her." But even the most unconditional love could suffer from neglect or abuse and become warped.

"I'm suddenly interested in attending the funeral," Phillipa claimed. "I hope my motor car is not fixed before then."

"Yes, the culprit might attend." As well as the committee ladies. Evie cringed. This would mark their first encounter since the afternoon tea fiasco. She hoped everyone remembered to bring along their manners.

Evie looked over at Tom. "I suppose it's now time for you to go out there and mug someone for their clothes." Since stepping into the shoes of Mr. Winchester, Tom had been procuring appropriate clothing without any effort whatsoever, almost as if he had access to a source of infinite abundance.

Tom drummed his fingers on the table. "That shouldn't be a problem. Did you get around to asking the ladies if they have an interest in gardening?"

As she looked away from Tom, Evie felt he didn't even have to try to wear the mark of confidence and success. He carried it with such ease, she had been having trouble remembering she employed him as her chauffeur.

"Heavens, no. With so much being said, it completely slipped my mind. Perhaps Mrs. Clarissa Penn can assist in this matter. Henrietta did well to engage her services as a spy. Although, she's bound to insist Mrs. Penn offered." Sighing, Evie added, "I suppose I should go check on Henrietta. After the committee ladies marched out of here, she went to lie down."

She found Henrietta in her room reading a book and drinking a cup of tea.

"I feel I ought to apologize for everyone's behavior today, Henrietta, including my own. I should not have allowed the discussion to get out of hand as it did."

"I doubt even the force of nature could have stopped Mrs. Hallesberry. As for the Vicar's wife…" Henrietta snorted. "She has a bee in her bonnet and I don't understand why. Perhaps we should speak with the Vicar. There might be trouble in paradise and Mrs. Ellington is taking it out on the rest of us, me in particular."

"She used to be so pleasant," Evie murmured.

"Yes," Henrietta agreed. "If I wanted to be unkind, I would say she suffered under the tyrannical hands of a man who treats her like a doormat and has now pushed her to the outer limits of her patience and tolerance forcing her to, as you would put it, blow her stack."

Evie sat on a chair opposite. "Henrietta, have you ever heard rumors about anyone carrying on?"

Henrietta gave an impish smile. "My dearest, rumors about people taking off with someone other than their spouse have always kept the mills grinding and I doubt they will ever stop."

Evie must have looked mystified. So much so, Henrietta leaned forward and patted her hand.

"You are a treasure."

"I feel I've been living under a rock," Evie admitted.

"Do you mean to say you have never heard of the Duchess of Devonshire?"

"Of course, I have. The Devonshire family own the grandest house in England." Evie clicked her fingers. "Chatsworth."

"Yes, but I am specifically referring to Georgiana Cavendish, Duchess of Devonshire."

Evie searched her mind for something intriguing she might have heard about the duchess.

"She was famous for her love affairs, among

other things, which escalated her fame to notoriety. Heavens, she even had a child with Charles, Earl Grey while she remained married to the Duke. If someone of her social standing carried on the way she did, imagine what someone else might think they could get away with." When Evie didn't respond, the dowager asked, "You think Mrs. Howard-Smith had been having an affair?" The dowager gasped.

"Why did you just do that?"

"I'm shocked," Henrietta admitted.

"But you just told me about the Duchess of Devonshire without even batting an eyelash."

"Yes, but her affair is so far removed from my current reality, I can take it with a grain of salt. This, on the other hand, is indeed shocking. Do you have someone in mind?" The dowager surged to her feet. "We must speak with Sara. "She gets out and about more than I do these days."

"I'll call her and invite her to dinner, something I shouldn't have to do if you had both remained living at Halton House."

Henrietta patted her hand again. "I think you are entitled to some time alone. Of course, if you insist, we will be only too happy to return." The dowager strode toward the door murmuring, "It feels strange to be invited back to one's own home."

Evie murmured right back, "I haven't extended the invitation yet."

14

“Dinner is the principal act of the day that can only be carried out in a worthy manner by people of wit and humor; for it is not sufficient just to eat at dinner. One has to talk with a calm and discreet gaiety. The conversation must sparkle… it must be delightfully suave with the sweetmeats of the dessert and become very profound with the coffee…”
- Alexandre Dumas

The drawing room, Halton House

“We must attack by stealth,” Henrietta suggested as they left the dining room and strode into the drawing room. “Take them out one by one.”

Evie sunk into her chair. “I feel responsible. Perhaps you should give me the opportunity to broker a peace.”

“That ship has sailed, Evangeline.” Henrietta accepted a drink from Edgar who, nodding, appeared to heartily approve of the dowager’s stalwart remark. “We have already made far too many concessions. It is time to take a stand.”

Evie sighed. “This is meant to be a fundraiser. Maybe if we focus on that, we would all come together…"

The dowager wouldn't hear of it. "I say we start with Mrs. Browning. On second thought, Mrs. Hallesberry has shown her true colors. Their land adjoins ours. To think, we have been neighbors all these years. I wouldn't be surprised if she has spent all this time plotting against us. Learning our weaknesses…"

"And what might those be?" Evie asked.

Henrietta lifted her chin. "Our unquestionable generosity. Think of everything we have done for this district."

Evie's head spun. The entire dinner conversation had revolved around the committee's wrongdoing, culminating in Henrietta's desire for blood.

Evie accepted a glass of port. "All I can say is that you should be careful what you wish for." Evie then proceeded to guide the conversation to a more mundane subject by asking, "Do any of you know if there are any new litters around? I would love to adopt a puppy."

Disregarding the question, the dowager said, "Sara agrees with me."

Oh, dear. That made it two against one.

Sara took a quick sip of her drink and, in her suave tone, declared, "We have reached a stalemate. They insist on organizing the event but they no longer have a venue for it. What's to be gained by persevering? I say we simply go ahead and put a solid plan into motion. We do have the advantage now. And an unshakable one at that."

"Yes," Henrietta agreed and then surprised everyone with a mellowed voice of reason. "However, we might be perceived as opportunists, eager to take advantage of an unfortunate death. The rebels might gain the sympathy vote."

"I doubt it will come to that," Sara offered. "At the end of the day, the guests will simply wish to have a good time."

The dowager gave it some thought and then turned her attention to Tom. Giving him a warm smile, she said, "You seem awfully quiet, Mr. Winchester."

"I'm afraid I can't be of much help to you. Dueling society hostesses remain out of my scope of experience."

"In other words, you wish to remain neutral."

Evie thought she heard Tom say he couldn't think of a safer place to be.

Henrietta gave a firm nod. "When all is said and done, we must remain true to our cause. I will organize the invitations in the morning." She cast her gaze around the drawing room as if challenging them to contradict her or provide a word of reproach.

Edgar broke the silence by announcing, "A telephone call for the Countess."

"Which one?" all three Countesses of Woodridge asked.

"Lady Henrietta Woodridge."

"Who could be calling me at this time of the evening and here, at Halton House?" the dowager asked without moving.

"There is only one way to find out, Henrietta. Would you like me to take the call?" Evie asked.

Henrietta took a pensive sip of her port and then set the glass down. "Oh, I suppose I should see who it is. For all we know, it might be urgent." Henrietta shivered and made her way to the door, saying, "I always dread these telephone calls. I remember back in 1877 a flyer made its way around stating persons using the telephone could converse miles apart, in precisely the same manner as though they were in the same room, yet I always find myself shouting into the contraption. I think we have all been fooled by its benefits. To think, when Queen Victoria had a demonstration from the inventor himself, she found herself much gratified and surprised by it, going so far as to purchase the instruments post-haste. I often wonder where we might be if she had found it disrupting to our social fabric."

When the dowager finally left to answer the call, everyone sat back in silence, almost as if relieved to finally have a moment of quiet.

It did not last.

Henrietta entered the drawing room and went to stand in the middle, turning to gather everyone's attention to her. "We are in the midst of a storm."

"Really?" Evie asked. "But it's been so sunny."

"I am not referring to the weather, my dear Evangeline. Doctor Browning has been seen rushing across the village."

Evie took a deep swallow. "Perhaps he is on his way to deliver a baby."

Henrietta gave a brisk shake of her head. "My butler took the liberty of telephoning me here with the news which he received from Doctor Browning's maid, the one who is rather keen on him. I'm not so sure I am keen on her but as I seem to be benefiting from the swift delivery of news, I am prepared to turn a blind eye. I don't really mean to imply there is something going on between the maid and my butler, at least, not that I know of."

Evie sat up. "Henrietta. The news."

"Oh, yes. Doctor Browning rushed off to attend to Mrs. Hallesberry who has been taken ill."

One of the committee ladies… who had attended afternoon tea at Halton House?

"I don't wish to alarm you, Evangeline. However, comparisons are being made."

So late in the evening? Evie took a deep swallow. "What type of comparisons?"

"Mrs. Howard-Smith had tea with you and later that night, she died. Mrs. Hallesberry also had tea with you and now she is drawing her last breath."

"Mamma. Must you be so morbidly dramatic?" Sara asked.

"My choice of expression has nothing to do with me. I am merely the messenger and those were the precise words passed on to me. The Countess of Woodridge has been labelled a poisoner. I wish we could have been spared this dilemma. Now only the very brave will attend the ball. Although, I expect most people will be curious enough to risk their lives…"

15

A fatal coincidence is called into question

The library, Halton House

"Mrs. Hallesberry manifested the same symptoms as Mrs. Howard-Smith," the detective confirmed.

Evie contained her frustration by gripping the armrests. Why couldn't the detective come straight out and tell her how the woman had died? How could she draw a line of defense if she didn't have all the details?

The detective held Evie's gaze for a moment and then looked down at his notebook. "That is not the only similarity in this case."

For once, Evie did not interrupt.

"From what I understand, Mrs. Hallesberry had afternoon tea here… at Halton House."

The detective's tact surprised Evie. He could easily have come straight out and said the deceased had sat to afternoon tea with her.

"Yes, she and some other ladies attended a tea party organized by Lady Woodridge."

The detective cleared his throat. "Which Lady Woodridge might that be?"

Thinking two could play at the game of evasion, Evie gave him a small smile. "The Countess of Woodridge, of course." She threw Tom a brief glance and saw him shake his head and roll his eyes.

The detective glanced around the library. Returning his attention to his notebook, something else appeared to catch his eye. He leaned sideways and reached for a book that had been left on a small table.

"A manual of poisonous plants," he read. "May I ask who has been reading this?"

Evie exchanged a quick look with Tom. "I have," they both answered at the same time.

"You both read it together?"

"As a matter of fact, yes." Evie leaned forward and took the book from the detective. "Since you have been reluctant to share information with us, we felt compelled to do some research."

"And what exactly led you to look into poisonous plants?" the detective asked.

"Deductive thinking. We were aware of the symptoms suffered by Mrs. Howard-Smith and concluded her death might have been brought about by some sort of poisonous substance."

"There are many poisons," the detective said. "Why plants?"

"Oh, now I remember." Evie gave him a satisfied smile. "You pointed us to the subject when you asked me if I gardened. In fact, you asked Phillipa Brady the same question."

"Indeed."

"Yes, indeed," Evie said. "Detective, are you, by any chance, suggesting I might be in some way responsible for Mrs. Hallesberry's death?"

"You must forgive me, my lady. At some point, coincidences tend to become suspicious. I believe we have reached that point."

Evie shifted to the edge of her chair. "Have you retraced her steps after she left Halton House?"

He gave a reluctant nod. "We questioned several local ladies, including the Vicar's wife. They all said Mrs. Hallesberry bid them farewell at your doorstep, after which, she made her way home."

"And?"

"She went home, my lady."

"Are you telling me their testimony is written in stone? Did any of them actually see Mrs. Hallesberry enter her house? Have you spoken to her household staff?"

The detective looked confused. Clearing his throat and appearing to regain control of himself, he said, "I would like to focus on the events which took place here. I am told you argued with Mrs. Hallesberry and threatened to have her thrown out and exposed as a conniving fraud."

Evie gasped. "I never. I would never. Who told you such a lie?"

"I am afraid I am not at liberty to divulge such information."

Tom surged to his feet and paced around the library, making several sweeps past the detective. Evie noticed every time he strode past him, his gaze dropped to the notebook the detective held.

She imagined Tom going through a process of collecting information as he went, one little bit at a time and piecing it together like a jigsaw puzzle in his mind.

Distracted, Evie lost herself in the thought. That seemed to pull her further away from the detective's chatter and she experienced a lapse in focus, trailing off to a happy moment earlier in the day when she had stretched and yawned, content to wake up to a new day and quite oblivious to what awaited her.

Confirmation of another death.

"Lady Woodridge."

Startled out of the reverie, Evie sat up.

"Everyone attending the tea said you were quite insistent Mrs. Hallesberry drink more of your tea, which happens to be a special blend."

"Oh, yes. I believe they all enjoyed it."

The detective read through more of his notes, and asked, "Did everyone drink from the same pot of tea?"

"I'm not sure. With a gathering of more than three guests, there is usually more than one teapot on the table. I would have to ask the butler."

"Would you mind doing that now?" the

detective asked.

Evie crossed the room and rang for Edgar who appeared within minutes.

"Yes, my lady. There were two teapots," he confirmed.

"Satisfied, detective?"

"Not quite. Did you happen to drink from the same teapot as Mrs. Hallesberry?"

"Yes, of course. It would have been the one nearest me." Putting two and two together, Evie gave him her most imperious look perfected over the years by observing Lady Henrietta Woodridge. "Are you trying to imply I poisoned Mrs. Hallesberry?"

"As I said, my lady, coincidences tend to become suspicious."

"Edgar. Who prepared the tea?"

"I believe I did, my lady."

"And did you poison Mrs. Hallesberry?"

"I believe I didn't, my lady."

Evie gave the detective a pointed look. "There. Are you satisfied now?"

"I do have one more request. Could you take me through the main topic of conversation?"

Tom came to a complete stop only to sink down on the nearest chair.

Oh, yea of little faith, Evie thought.

***

"I believe I am now officially a suspect," Evie declared.

"Did you do that on purpose?" Tom asked. "The detective appeared to be perfectly satisfied with your responses but then you had to launch into a diatribe about wasting police resources on wrongful accusations and, in particular, on an innocent bystander."

"Is this where you tell me my grandmother warned you about my colorful temper?"

"She did mention it but had difficulty explaining it. Now I understand what she meant when she described you as being somewhat flighty."

Instead of taking offence, Evie smiled. "Is that really how she described me?"

"To quote your grandmother, "When in a fit of rage, my granddaughter has been known to induce a state of histrionics and go off on a tangent, usually pursuing a subject in complete opposition to the source of her exasperation" end quote."

"Dearest granny," Evie sighed. "I inherited the histrionic trait from her. Not that she'd ever admit it, but she had aspired to go on the stage and then she met my grandfather." Smiling, she asked, "How would you rate my performance?"

"Having been forewarned, I had expected an outburst of emotions. Instead, you delivered a subdued attack focusing on the inner workings of the police force." Tom smiled and finished by saying, “I feel short-changed.”

“My apologies. Over the years, I have acquired a certain degree of maturity but can you honestly believe the man’s audacity, suggesting I had quarreled with Mrs. Hallesberry?”

Laughing, Tom said, “I believe he tried to bait you.”

And she’d fallen for it. Hook, line and sinker.

“Why do you think he did that? Surely, he’s not hoping to force a fake confession out of me.”

Tom clasped his hands and shrugged. “Mrs. Browning has been your fiercest critic. Perhaps she elaborated her tale so you would appear to have just cause to act against Mrs. Hallesberry.”

Aha! Mrs. Browning. “I wondered if you were trying to decipher the detective’s notes.”

“He had underlined her name,” Tom confirmed. “Twice. He even added an exclamation mark.”

“I can’t think why the doctor’s wife would have it in for me. I’ve only just met her.” Evie sprung to her feet and crossed over to the window. “I’m beginning to think this really is a rebellion against the titled gentry. They have been pushing for a democracy where none can possibly exist. What will they do next? Tear down any village signs with the name Halton written on them?”

Despite Henrietta raising the alarm and suggesting something had happened to someone in the village, when Evie had retired to her room the previous evening, she had entertained hopes that all would be well. However, her hopes had been dashed. Soon after settling down to her breakfast, news had reached her…

Mrs. Hallesberry.

Dead.

Even now, the news continued to spin around her mind.

"And yet, the only victims are the very people who wish to oust you from your lofty station in life," Tom continued. "The committee ladies should let that be a warning not to cross you. Either that, or they should politely decline any offer of tea from you…"

Evie knew she should have laughed, but she really failed to see the humor in the picture he'd painted. Wringing her hands, she strode around the library. "Two deaths. Both women succumbed to the same symptoms. Are we to assume they both died in the same manner, which in turn means they were both killed by the same person?"

Tom gave a reluctant shrug. "I don't see any harm in making those assumptions."

"So, what else did Mrs. Hallesberry and Mrs. Howard-Smith have in common?"

"The same enemy?" Tom suggested.

"Yes, but something made them a target."

Upon hearing the news about Mrs. Howard-Smith and discussing the apparent veil of secrecy favored by the committee ladies, Evie had proceeded to entertain the possibility of an illicit affair.

Could both women have been having an affair?

They both stared at each other without blinking or saying anything until Evie broke the silence. "No. Really?"

"It's possible."

Could they have both shared the same lover?

Evie swung away and strode to the window but the view failed to provide any clarity. "I'm not sure I'm entirely comfortable following that train of thought. Although it would narrow down the suspects."

Two women. One lover.

"Did you have someone in mind?" Tom asked.

"Yes, the Lothario responsible for luring two women into an affair or, assuming he also has a wife, his spouse. And, if I can take the liberty to engage my imagination, I would also consider a third suspect. Someone who is aware of what has been going on and does not approve."

"I meant, did you have someone in particular in mind?"

"No, my suspicions are far too general. But that's something we can work with."

Three possible suspects. Yes, they could work with that…

The lover. His wife. Or… a shadowy third suspect with strong opinions on the matter.

"For someone who is outside of their comfort zone, you appear to do some impressive creative thinking," Tom remarked. "Make that, deductive thinking."

Evie gave him a bright smile. "Yes, and now I'm rather pleased with myself."

Tom came to stand next to her. "What inspired you to think along those lines?"

Shrugging, Evie said, "The detective has been short on information so he has left us no choice. I had a spark of an idea and I went with it." She resumed looking out of the window. "I can't help feeling we are quite insulated here."

Tom gave her a brisk smile. "So, there are no skeletons in the Woodridge closets?"

"None that I am aware of and now that you mention it, I might have to spend a rainy day searching through the house for hidden journals or love letters."

Tom crossed his arms and, leaning against the window, watched her. "Meanwhile, what do you propose doing about the rumors floating about?"

"I suppose they'll die down eventually. Silence will be my best line of defense. The police are busy retracing both victims' steps. That should distract the gossips." She stopped to think through the last few days. Her gaze fixed on a tree standing tall and majestic among a copse of smaller ones.

"You just had an idea," Tom murmured.

Surprised at his insightful remark, she looked

at him. “How could you possibly tell?”

“Your eyes brightened.”

“I’ll have to take your word for that.”

His eyebrows drew downward. “Are you going to share your idea?”

“A part of me wishes to stay right out of this imbroglio and go on as if nothing has happened.” She watched his jaw muscles at work and sensed his growing impatience.

“You’re going to make me beg.”

“If I tell you, will I become no better than the average person who spreads rumors about?”

“No. Now, tell me.”

“There’s one man who stands out and I have personally witnessed his effect on women. The local stud. Charlie Timms.”

16

Evie inspected the hat Caro had selected for her. The band around it appeared to be secure. As did the small black cat curled up and looking quite pleased with itself. She twitched it to make sure it would stay in place. When it did, she inspected the inside of the hat. Everything looked to be in order.

She then proceeded to cast a critical eye over her leather gloves, giving each finger a slight tug to test the seams. Finding nothing wrong with them, she set them aside and tried to think what else her maid might have sabotaged.

Her eyes widened and she looked down at the heels of her shoes. A dozen scenarios which included her heels being sawed off crossed her mind. She moved her ankles one way and the other. Again, everything appeared to be in fine working order.

Sighing with relief, Evie decided Caro had abandoned her deliberate or unconscious wilful tampering of her clothes.

Yet Caro didn't look pleased.

"Is there something I should be aware of, Caro?"

"No, milady."

Caro's curt reply set off alarm bells. "What now, Caro? Tell me what's on your mind and I'll try to fix the problem."

"It's nothing really…"

"Usually when you say it's nothing, it turns out to be quite something. Do you plan to ambush me with your grievances?"

"Milady! I would never… I mean, not deliberately."

"Yes, yes. I know. Last time you said you didn't know what had come over you. Can we try to prevent that from happening again?"

Caro gave a small nod. "Well… There has been some talk downstairs about you getting a puppy."

Evie brightened. "Oh, yes. Has someone heard news about a litter?"

Caro's lips pressed into a mulish expression. "If there is room for a puppy then surely there is room for a little seven-year-old boy. There, I've said it."

Oh, dear…

"Caro. I will make sure to let Seth know how much you love him, because clearly you do."

Caro gave an eager nod. "He is an adorable little boy."

"Have you considered what your strong

emotions might be trying to tell you?"

"I'm not sure I know what you mean, milady."

"I believe there is someone for everyone and you might not have found that special someone, but you will."

Caro's eyebrows performed a little dance and then settled into a straight line. "You think I'm pining for love?"

"You probably are and that's why you are fretting so much over Seth." Lowering her voice, Evie asked, "Has someone caught your eye?"

Caro looked down at her hands and then away into the distance.

"There is someone!" Evie shifted in her chair and gave Caro a nod of encouragement. When her maid hesitated, Evie found herself entertaining the oddest thought. What if Caro had fallen for Tom? Caro had looked somewhat aggrieved when Tom, the chauffeur, had stepped into the shoes of independently wealthy Mr. Tom Winchester. Evie assumed her maid would perceive the change as a social barrier she would never be able to cross.

Caro's cheeks colored. "You're making me blush."

"Where did you meet him?" Evie encouraged.

Shaking her head, Caro said, "I first caught sight of him in the village. My mother always tells me to look beyond surface appearances…"

Relief swept through Evie. Not Tom… "Oh, yes… Beauty is in the eye of the beholder."

"Well, that's just it, milady. He is terribly handsome. So much so, I feel quite plain."

"Oh, no. You must never feel plain, dear Caro." Surging to her feet, Evie nodded. "You need a new dress. Go into the village today and find something special and put it on my account."

"I'm not sure what good that will do. He is so very good looking..."

Evie's smile wavered. "Caro… What is this human personification of Adonis' name?"

***

Evie pulled on her gloves and stated, "It's personal now."

Tom gave her a lifted eyebrow look that spoke of incredulity. "Of course it is. You are being held responsible for two deaths. Not officially, otherwise the police would have hauled you away. But the general consensus seems to be prevailing at the moment. Guilty until proven innocent."

"Are you quite finished poking fun at me?" Evie asked, her tone full of indignation.

Tom smiled. "Yes, I think so…"

Shaking her head, she explained, "Caro is infatuated with the village Lothario, Charlie Timms. He must be held accountable for his actions." Settling into the passenger seat of the red roadster she waved her hand, "Drive on, please."

"Yes, ma'am." Once they cleared the gates, he asked, "Which way?"

"To Hollyhock Farm. I am going to confront Charlie Timms and force him to admit to his debauchery. Assuming it is him."

Tom chuckled under his breath. "And how do you propose making him admit to his rakish pursuits?"

"I'll figure it out. And… please don't mock me. Meanwhile, you could engage your resourceful mind and try to come up with ideas. My maid's honor is at stake, not to mention her heart and my clothes."

"Your clothes?"

"Yes, I need Caro to be happy or I'll be facing a hefty dressmaker's bill. Who knows what my wretched maid will do if she doesn't find someone to take her mind off Seth."

They drove the rest of the way in silence until Evie wondered out loud, "The neighbor I saw up in a tree might be able to help us."

"The neighbor you imagined seeing. It might have been a cat," Tom suggested.

"No, I had the distinct impression we were being watched. Even after we abandoned the idea of anyone answering the bell and walked around the building to look at the orchard. If Charlie Timms has been carrying on with one or more women, then I believe the neighbor will have something to say about it. In fact, I would bet anything they are eager to share what they know. It's to do with the force of human nature."

Glancing at her, Tom asked, "Does this mean you have been dipping into those books you pulled out of the shelves?"

To Evie's surprise, she had read through an entire book only to start again as most of it had been quite difficult to understand. "Yes, my attention has been engaged. I find the subject of the human mind and behaviors intriguing. I'm hoping the third reading will open my mind to a better understanding of the subject."

"Third?"

"I skimmed through it the first time." Evie huffed out a breath. "The author uses too many words to get to the point." Another huff had her admitting, "I seem to be a slow learner."

"I'm sure you'll get the hang of it eventually. By the way," Tom said as he slowed down to take a bend in the road, "Meg Harrison came through with more information from her friend who works at Witford Hall."

Evie remembered Tom had asked the pub's maid to make further inquiries for them…

"Mrs. Howard-Smith returned to Witford Hall rather late. Her husband had gone into London to attend a dinner and he didn't return until much later. According to the maid, Mrs. Howard-Smith asked for a cup of tea and then went straight to bed."

So… The husband had been conveniently

away on the evening she died. "Had she already been complaining of nausea when she arrived?"

"No. The maid said she took in the cup of tea and half an hour later, Mrs. Howard-Smith rang for her. That's when she became ill. Several hours later, her condition worsened and they called for the doctor."

Evie gasped. "But that means someone within her household could have poisoned her."

"Maybe. Then again, she did go straight to bed so she might already have been feeling ill."

True. Also, if someone within her household had poisoned her, they would have to rethink their theory of the same person killing both women.

"Did the maid know where she'd been?"

"No, but she told Meg Mrs. Howard-Smith always took advantage of her husband's trips."

"And?"

"That's all she said. We can assume she meant Mrs. Howard-Smith took the liberty to go out by herself."

To meet her lover?

When Hollyhock Farm came into view, Tom slowed down and asked, "Well, have you come up with a plan?"

Evie bit the edge of her lip. "Not really. I'm obsessing about something else. The detective must have known all along about Mrs. Howard-Smith's late arrival as well as the tea her maid took up to her."

Tom gave a pensive nod. "You're annoyed because he let you stew in your own juices."

Yes. He'd made her think she had become a suspect. "If he had this information, why did he feel compelled to question me?" Seeing Charlie Timms emerging from his house, Evie shrugged. "Never mind all that. Put your thinking cap on."

"Just so we are clear, you suspect Charlie Timms of wooing local women and then poisoning them."

"Yes."

"How did we end up following this train of thought?" Tom asked.

"Let me think." Evie tapped her chin. "Oh, yes. We decided the committee ladies were safeguarding a secret and that led us to conclude it had to be a secret liaison."

"Yes, but why Charlie Timms?"

"You'll know once you meet him. He is… Well… He is quite good looking. Are you about to suggest we might be barking up the wrong tree?"

Shaking his head, Tom said, "I'm trying to pull away and look at the bigger picture but I seem to be caught up in your theory. However, do we really believe two women were having an affair with the same man?"

"I think it might be best to suspend all disbelief and open our minds up to any possibility." Tom didn't look convinced. "I will not sit by and watch my maid's heart be broken by a callous rogue."

"Well then, we should catch up with Charlie Timms."

They followed the path he'd taken. The farm buildings were lined up to one side and on the other, beyond the neatly trimmed hedges, there were fields with various crops growing on them. Finally, they strode into the stable yard where they found Charlie Timms inspecting a horse and giving it an occasional pat. When he saw them, he removed his cap and nodded.

"That's a fine looking horse, Mr. Timms."

"Thank you, milady."

Evie introduced him to Tom, saying, "I've been telling Mr. Winchester all about your stud services." In every sense of the word, Evie thought.

"Well, if you're looking for a horse, this is the place to come. His Lordship here has the finest temperament. He's been siring the best hunters around."

Evie ran her hand over the horse's mane. "We were actually wondering who your clients might be."

Charlie Timms brushed his hand across his chin. "I would have to say most of the locals with stables."

That would put him in contact with just about everyone in the county, Evie thought. She needed to narrow it all down. But how?

Evie looked about her and smiled. "I'm so

glad we came out today. We've been spending endless hours in the library and missing out on this bright, sunny weather." Her smile faded and as she spoke she watched Charlie Timms for any signs that might give him away. "I suppose that's not the worst that can happen. There are some people who won't be enjoying this fine weather… I recently had tea with Mrs. Howard-Smith and she told me how much she enjoyed riding in the hunt." In actual fact, Evie had no idea if Mrs. Howard-Smith had enjoyed riding. "I guess she won't be doing much of that."

Charlie Timms looked into the distance.

"Did she happen to own one of your horses?"

His mouth firmed and he gave a barely perceptible nod. "She did."

"Of course, you would have heard about her unfortunate death."

His eyes lowered slightly. "Yes, it caught everyone by surprise."

Evie's patience paid off when he took a deep swallow.

Turning her attention to His Lordship, she gave him a pat and lowered her voice. "In fact, you knew her very well."

"I'm sure I don't know what you are referring to, milady."

Her mind provided her with a hunch and she went with it. "A few days ago, when I drove out here with the agent, I saw Mrs. Howard-Smith's car pulling away. Of course, it makes sense now.

Her husband had gone into town…" She only assumed the car she'd seen had belonged to Mrs. Howard-Smith. When Charlie Timms didn't contradict her, she decided her instinct had been right. She then decided that hadn't been the only time the car had driven out this way. "So, she rushed out here to be with you. Isn't that what happened?" Evie didn't wait for him to answer. She stroked His Lordship and added, "The night she died, she came to you."

"I told her it had to stop," he whispered, his voice carrying a surprising hint of emotion. "But she wouldn't listen."

Evie slanted her gaze toward him and saw his eyes had lost their focus.

Tom took a step forward. She wondered if he wanted to take up a position of advantage just in case Charlie Timms tried something.

"Did you tell the police about her visits?" Evie asked.

When he looked up, she saw his eyes harbored a storm of emotions.

"I couldn't." He shook his head. "Her reputation… Even now." He gave another shake of his head. "No one can know."

That struck Evie as odd. Why would he care about her reputation? Because he'd actually carcd about her?

Deciding to give her instinct another try, she said, "And there was also Mrs. Hallesberry. And now they are both dead." She gave him long enough to deny it, but he didn't. "What do you think the police will do if they find out they were both having an affair with you?"

"I didn't kill them." His fingers tightened around his cap. "I didn't."

17

Relieved not to be the guest of honor

Parish Church near Witford Hall

"Arriving at a funeral service in a roadster seems inappropriate."

"I don't feel the same way," Tom remarked. "In fact, it gives me a feeling of joyous affirmation for everything life has to offer. We're alive and we must make the best of it while we can."

Evie nodded. "You're quite right. In fact, you've managed to convert me to your way of thinking. The same can't be said for everyone who has just turned their heads to watch our arrival. I think they disapprove. Either that, or they are surprised to see me here. This is not how I imagined letting everyone know I had returned to Berkshire." Glancing at Tom, Evie rolled her eyes. "Try not to look so cheerful."

"My apologies. I'd just been thinking what I will tell your grandmother when she next asks what you have been up to."

"She actually checks up on me?"

"Regularly. You are her heiress."

"Next time you correspond with her, please check with me. I wouldn't want us to provide her with contrasting accounts."

Tom laughed. "Are you afraid she'll catch you out in a lie?"

"Not me. I'm her granddaughter. She's bound to take my word over yours."

He smiled. "I wouldn't be so sure about that."

Evie spent a few moments admiring the local church which stood on a hill near a babbling brook. "She will have a lovely view and her family won't have far to travel if they wish to visit.

Tom brushed his hand across his face. "She's dead."

"Must you be such a pessimist?"

"I prefer to think of myself as a realist."

Evie let the remark slide thinking she didn't wish to find herself having to justify the two years she had spent in deep mourning… "Henrietta said we should be able to see Witford Hall from here." Evie pointed toward a copse of trees. "There. To the right of those trees. It's quite imposing."

Tom agreed with a nod. "I still can't quite understand how a country with such a small land mass can accommodate so many large estates." Tom brought the motor car to a stop. "I see the committee ladies are here."

Evie scanned the congregation milling around the church yard and wondered if the killer stood among them. The three remaining members of the committee stood together, shoulder to shoulder. Mrs. Clarissa Penn, Henrietta's spy, appeared to be in shock. Her eyes looked wide and her lips slightly parted.

"Have you decided what you're going to do about Charlie Timms?" Tom asked.

Since Charlie had admitted to having affairs with both women, Evie knew she should have gone straight to the police with the information.

Despite her efforts to extricate a full confession, he had refused to name anyone else he might be involved with. Evie wanted to believe him. She hoped she could. She had delayed passing the information onto the police mostly because she had felt swayed by Charlie Timms' concern for the women's reputations, even after death. Tossing and turning during the night hadn't helped. What if he had only been looking after his own interests?

"Do you think Charlie Timms is afraid he will suffer consequences from being unmasked as the local Lothario?" Evie wondered out loud. "Everyone would stop buying horses from him. He would probably have to move away."

"I'm surprised you don't wish him to pay for his sins."

"Why would I want him to pay for his affairs? It's none of my business, I'm sure."

"You're a woman. You're supposed to disapprove."

Evie turned to look at Tom. "I can't tell if you're being serious or not." Seeing the edges of his eyes crinkling with amusement, she shook her head. "You're making fun of me."

"Actually, I'm probably poking fun at myself. Most men tend to generalize women but I'm finding it difficult to do it with you."

Evie couldn't help smiling. In most matters, she wished to make up her own mind rather than allow herself to be swept along with the general consensus. If that made her different, then so be it. Also…

She rather liked the idea of Tom seeing her in a different light.

"I am shocked by the affairs but I don't see the point of casting aspersions. Each to his own. He didn't have the affairs by himself. And while he should have known better than to become involved with married women, they should have known better too." She gave it some more thought and added, "I should be annoyed by the aftermath. After all, I have been dragged into it all simply because I tried to intervene. Remind me never to encourage peaceful resolutions." Evie lifted her chin. "I have learned my lesson. Sometimes, there is simply no swaying people from their disagreeable manners."

"So, will you tell the police about Charlie Timms?"

"I might try to strike a deal. Surely there is nothing to be gained by dragging everyone's name through the mud and making the affairs public. However, the police need to speak with everyone who came into contact with both women. They might find a new lead."

"Does that mean you believe Charlie Timms is innocent of killing them?"

Evie sighed. "He admitted to having the affairs. If he'd been guilty of killing them, I think he might have tried to deny even knowing them." His acquaintance with both women put Charlie Timms in a perilous position and Evie didn't want to be the one to throw him to the wolves, certainly not without good reason. She would decide what to do after the service.

"Here come the dowagers," Tom said.

The chauffeured driven car came to a stop beside Tom's roadster.

Henrietta's chauffeur, Hobson, stepped out and held the door open for Henrietta, Sara and Phillipa who had expressed an interest in attending the service.

When they emerged, they immediately sent their gazes skating over everyone congregated outside the church.

"It's almost as if we are all compelled to see who remains standing," Evie mused.

Tom came around and opened the passenger door for her. "Thank you. Oh… Would you mind doing me a favor?" Evie didn't wait for him to answer. "I'm going to turn around very slowly and I'd like you to see if there is anything out of place."

"Dare I ask?"

Evie turned and sighed. "It is rather a long story."

"From experience, funerals tend to inspire people into reminiscing. We all know how you felt about Mrs. Howard-Smith but if you tell me your tale, then it will appear as though you are recounting a fond memory about the lady."

"Fine, I'll tell you, but I'm sure you'll find it all too silly. Caro is cross with me and she has been taking it out on my clothes. She shows all signs of being remorseful but that doesn't mean she will stop laying siege to my wardrobe."

Tom chortled. "I'm trying to imagine it but I'm failing."

Huffing out a breath, Evie said, "In one instance, the flowers on my hat were plucked clean of their petals. I fear she is planning her next assault and will try to catch me by surprise."

"Wait a minute… Is this why you were losing your feathers the other night?"

"Yes. Caro's handy work. If we didn't get on so well, I'd have a good mind to send her on her way. Imagine if I did something truly wicked. I'd have to sleep with one eye open."

"And what exactly did you do to deserve such creative attention from your maid?"

"Nothing… I mean, nothing I find terrible but Caro seems to think I am heartless because I sent Seth Halton to a preparatory school."

"He is only seven," Tom murmured.

"Oh, for heaven's sake. Not you too."

Laughing, Tom looked away and asked, "Is that Everett Townsend?"

"The pineapple man? Where?"

"Near the grieving committee members. Correct me if I'm wrong, but it looks to me as if he is eavesdropping on their conversation."

Evie had to agree. Everett Townsend had the look of a man pretending to be interested in a statue while leaning slightly toward the group of women.

"I wonder if he would be prepared to share what he overhears?" Evie asked.

"And I wonder why he is even trying to listen in on the conversation," Tom remarked. "What does he hope to gain?"

When Henrietta and Sara joined them, Evie asked, "Do you recognize anyone?"

"Yes. Most of those in attendance, but I do spy some new faces," Henrietta said. "When you are young, you are likely to extend your circle of acquaintances by attending balls and soirees. Eventually, you begin to attend funerals. As time progresses, you find yourself attending less balls and more services for the dearly departed. Strangely, the circle of acquaintances then begins to decrease."

"Make the best of it, Henrietta. I doubt you'll be meeting many new people at our tea parties."

"My dear, I never knew you to be such a

pessimist. I'm sure people will find something new to talk about soon. Perhaps you should focus on creating a distraction…"

Oh, yes. That would do the trick, Evie thought. Create a new scandal.

"We should circulate and keep our focus on odd behavior," Evie suggested. "And anyone who appears to not belong here. Or… maybe someone who looks uncomfortable and ready to make a run for it."

Henrietta cast her glance around. "You do that, Evangeline, while I'll keep an eye out for the guilty looking ones."

"Isn't that what I just said?"

Phillipa joined the group. "Is it just me, or is everyone looking about as if searching for a culprit?"

"We are," Evie agreed. "Everyone is intrigued."

She had told both Sara and Henrietta about Charlie Timms, making them swear they wouldn't spread the story around. Phillipa also knew about him. She had seen Charlie Timms outside the tea room and she hadn't been at all surprised by the news, agreeing he would be the most likely candidate to have lured two women to their ruin. She also doubted he would have it in him to kill them.

Evie wondered if his magnetism somehow charmed women into believing he could do no wrong.

How much trouble would she get into if she didn't pass on the information to the police? And if she did tell them about Charlie Timms, would the police be discreet about it? She would hate to be responsible for blemishing anyone's reputation without being able to provide absolute proof of wrongdoing.

So far, they had two unfortunate souls who'd fallen prey to a killer and had also been carrying on an affair with Charlie Timms. As the inspector had said, too many coincides become suspicious. Regardless, Evie thought they needed to dig deeper and find a reasonable motive.

Turning, Evie saw a familiar motor car. She had seen one just like it not long ago. Putting her hand on Tom's sleeve, she said, "How would you feel about engaging that chauffeur in conversation and finding out who the owner of that motor car is?"

Tom gave her a brisk smile. "I would be delighted as I'm sure that's the answer you expected."

"Well, yes. Thank you." She'd had a hunch about the motor car and had used it to get Charlie Timms to admit he'd been having an affair. Confirmation of the car's owner would be something solid to take to the inspector. Although, it still wouldn't point the finger of guilt at Charlie Timms. Only a solid motive would do that. Of course, he could just be a cold-blooded murderer who didn't need a reason to kill.

"Do you have any last-minute instructions for us?" Henrietta asked.

"I'm sure I don't need to remind you the Howard-Smith family is burying one of their own today so we should take care to avoid antagonizing anyone here."

Henrietta's slightly lifted eyebrows suggested she held a different opinion.

"Do you have something to add, Henrietta?"

"I'm not sure I dare to since you just now told me to mind my manners."

Evie gave Henrietta an impish smile. "You know I meant well. I only wish to avoid involving the Woodridge family in a scandal."

"And yet you find yourself caught up in this web of intrigue. Your very presence here is bound to set everyone talking about you. I wouldn't be surprised if you are turned away at the church steps."

Oh, she hadn't thought of that.

"I shouldn't worry too much about it," Henrietta offered. "The committee ladies are causing quite a distraction with their whimpering. They might be wondering which one of them will be next."

"Is that supposed to comfort me?"

"Well, if you wish to play it safe, you might want to lower your head as we enter the church. And try to look contrite."

18

“I must say, it has been quite some time since I last saw a service so well attended,” Henrietta observed. “I would be inclined to say it does Mrs. Howard-Smith credit, however, I fear most people came expecting to witness a spectacle.”

Turning slightly, Evie caught sight of Detective Inspector O’Neill standing near a column. Had he come to make an arrest or did he wish to merely observe?

A hushed murmur swept through the church. She hadn’t been the only one to notice him. A discreet glance around confirmed he had not brought his constables. Evie hoped that meant he would not be arresting anyone today. At least, not here.

Tom joined them just as the organist began playing the opening hymn.

“Abide With Me,” Henrietta murmured. “What an odd choice of hymn. If she didn’t abide in life, what hope will she have of doing so in the afterlife?”

Evie waited until the hymn ended to prompt Tom. "Well?" she whispered.

"The car belongs to the Howard-Smith family."

Evie stared straight ahead. Her suppositions about the affair between Mrs. Howard-Smith and Charlie Timms had sounded so far-fetched, even after Charlie had confirmed it, she had struggled to believe it. And yet, she had seen the woman's car driving away from Hollyhock Farm with her own eyes.

The local stud had claimed he had tried to end the affair. He had sounded sincere but what if that had been part of his arsenal of weapons to maintain his innocence?

Evie couldn't claim to have any experience with suave men. She'd spoken with Charlie and had found him charming, in a rustic sort of way. Even if he hadn't said a word, she would have been captivated by his good looks.

Had he simply told her a convincing lie to save his own neck?

She shifted in her seat, suddenly feeling uncomfortable with the idea of eating out of anyone's hands.

Evie spent most of the service trying to come up with a motive and more suspects. As ludicrous as it sounded, she played around with the idea of a third affair with a woman so enraged by Charlie Timms' philandering, she decided to get rid of her competition.

The more she thought about it, the more absurd it sounded and yet, she wanted to share it with Tom, but everyone had fallen into a silent prayer. Even a whispered murmur would have drawn attention to her.

Slanting her gaze, she looked at Mrs. Browning.

She too had been held enthralled by the sight of Charlie Timms.

As a doctor's wife, she might have access to dangerous substances. Evie sat up. They'd been having so many committee meetings, she would also have had the perfect opportunity to put a nefarious plan into action.

Could she be the third woman?

If only the police would share more information. Both victims had left Evie's house in the afternoon and had then fallen ill at night. Whatever had been used to kill them would need several hours to take effect.

When Mrs. Browning glanced her way again, Evie made a mental note. Whatever happened over the next few days, she would not, under any circumstance, invite Mrs. Browning to tea.

As the service continued, Evie caught several mourners looking her way. Their expressions remained blank so she had no way of knowing what they hoped to see. But she could imagine them wondering if she'd been responsible for the deaths.

A nudge from Henrietta alerted her to the

presence of several women. “All looking across the aisle and toward the new widower,” Henrietta whispered.

At some point, Evie thought, they would all have to agree they had attended the service for all the wrong reasons. And to think, they had another one to attend in a few days’ time.

***

“I have a new suspect,” Evie declared as they strode away from the graveside and made their way to their respective vehicles.

Everyone turned to face her.

“Mrs. Browning. As the doctor’s wife she would have access to strong medication. If misused, I’m sure some could prove to be fatal.”

She watched everyone’s eyebrows curve up in surprise.

Pressing her hand to her chest, Henrietta asked, “That’s what you were thinking about inside the church? It’s almost sacrilegious, I’m sure.”

“Says the person who kept pointing out prospective husband hunters,” Evie accused lightly.

“I was merely trying to keep my spirits up. When you reach my age, you realize you are one step closer to the end and there’s no turning back or slowing down time.” Henrietta shivered. “I do hope someone gets married soon. I should like to attend a wedding and toast someone's good health and happiness. All this commiserating is dreadfully fatiguing." Looking toward Witford Hall, Henrietta sighed.

"If you're not up to going to the house," Sara said, "we can give it a miss."

"That would be highly uncivilized, Sara. We must pay our respects to the family. It is our duty. A Woodridge needs to put in an appearance and I can tell Evangeline is trying to find an excuse not to attend, so the task is left to us."

"I… I haven't said anything. Fine. Yes, Tom and I will give it a miss. I would like to have another word with Charlie Timms."

"You do that," Henrietta said. "Sara and I will do our best to champion your cause and dissuade anyone who dares to from thinking ill of you."

Evie thanked her with a smile. "I strongly advice you play it safe and steer clear of Mrs. Browning. At this point, I don't know if she's a prospective victim or the instigator of all these poisonings."

"I will go along too," Phillipa offered. "It will give me a chance to see Witford Hall from the inside." She shrugged. "What can I say? I'm still a tourist here and quite curious about all these large houses."

"Countess of Woodridge."

All three women turned to see Everett Townsend approaching them.

As they exchanged greetings and general

remarks about the turnout at the service, Evie bided her time, waiting for the appropriate moment to ask if he had overheard anything useful. However, Everett spared her the task.

"You might think this rather morbid, but I overheard a conversation I thought you might find interesting."

"Oh, do tell," Henrietta encouraged.

Glancing over his shoulder, he leaned in. "The committee ladies are getting jittery."

"Let me guess," Evie said, "they think one of them will be next."

"Why… Yes. I suppose you figured it out."

Evie decided to tell a small fib, "I think we're all entertaining the same concerns." His lifted eyebrow look suggested he might have reason to challenge her remark. "Then again, everyone seems intent on pointing the finger at me. By the way, would you like to come to tea?"

Everett straightened and Evie half expected him to take a step back.

"Would you accept a rain check?" he asked. "I have been rather absentminded lately and couldn't really tell you when I'll be free."

"Yes, of course. We would be delighted to have you over at any time. You know, I have my own special blend of tea. Everyone seems to be enjoying it."

This time, he did take a step back and, making his excuses, he left.

"Evangeline. I believe you enjoyed that far too

much," Henrietta chastised.

"Oh, perhaps a little." Watching Everett hurry away, she said, "I have a good mind to suspect him if for no other reason than… Well, he is the least likely suspect, which strikes me as the perfect ruse." Evie tilted her head in thought. "Yes, I believe I have a new suspect. Is he married?" She had been so preoccupied with everything going on around her, she hadn't bothered to ask.

"He is a widower," Henrietta said.

"Oh, do we know how his wife died?"

"A riding accident." Henrietta gave a pensive nod. "The more I think about it, the more I come to believe we would all fare better if we relied on our own two feet to get about."

"Tell that to someone with one leg," Sara murmured.

As they continued making their way to their vehicles, Evie wondered if they should try to question Charlie Timms' neighbor. She had been spying from the tree for a reason.

"Is this another hunch of yours?" Tom asked. "Sounds to me like you are giving Charlie too much leeway."

"I'd like to give him the opportunity to step up and talk to the police on his own volition. If anything, I'm more worried about there being a third lover."

"You're referring to Mrs. Browning."

Evie waved to the others. "Yes."

"What about the other two committee members?"

"Suspect the Vicar's wife? That would be ungodly."

"And Mrs. Penn?"

"She's one of ours." At least, she hoped so. Evie settled into the passenger seat. Waiting for Tom to start the car and get them on the way, she straightened her skirt. Finding a loose thread, she gave it a light tug and watched in horror as the hem of her skirt came completely undone. "Oh, dear."

Caro!

19

Adopt the pace of nature: her secret is patience
– Ralph Waldo Emerson

The Orchard

Tom stepped away from the gate, saying, "Surprise. Surprise. No one is home."

Evie nudged her head. "I beg to differ." Glancing along the high wall that enclosed the small cottage, Evie set her gaze on the tree. She could just make out a shape. "Hello," she called out and wanted to add they came in peace and didn't mean any harm, but she thought the woman might call her out on it. She felt almost certain they were being observed by a woman because she thought she'd seen a mop of bronze curls.

"You're trespassing."

Aha! Evie turned and gave Tom a bright smile. Introducing herself, Evie apologized for the intrusion. Although, in her opinion, the couldn't possibly be trespassing when they were still on the other side of the wall. Also… Strictly speaking, they were standing on Woodridge land.

"I'm Evie Parker, Countess of Woodridge. May I ask to whom I'm speaking?"

After a long pause, the woman said, "Elizabeth Young… milady." After another pause, she added, "Begging your pardon, milady. If I'd known it was you, I would have answered the bell."

They heard the rustling of leaves and a thump which might have been Elizabeth Young landing on the ground. A moment later, the gate opened.

Smiling at the young woman, Evie introduced Tom. To her surprise, Elizabeth invited them inside her cottage.

They were led through to a front parlor furnished with lovely pieces that must have been handed down from generation to generation. At a guess, Evie thought Elizabeth couldn't be older than twenty-five. She offered them tea and must have had a kettle on the fire because it only took her a few moments to prepare a tray.

Curiosity prompted Evie to ask, "Do you live here alone?"

Elizabeth gave a stiff nod and gestured to the chairs by the fireplace. A cabinet on the far side of the room displayed a surprising number of silver pieces such as might be seen in large manor houses.

"My parents were both taken by the Spanish flu and my brother never came back from the war."

"I am so sorry to hear that." It seemed

everyone had been scarred in one way or another. "Your parents lived here?" Even before Elizabeth could answer, Evie saw a collection of photographs on a small side table. "May I?"

Elizabeth gave a tentative nod. "Those are my parents."

The woman looked like a lady. If Evie had to guess, she'd think Elizabeth Young was well connected. Narrowing her gaze, she studied the background on the picture which appeared to be a grand house. "Was this their wedding day?"

Elizabeth looked at her without blinking. "At my grandfather's house. He is Baron Craigstone."

That made Elizabeth an Honorable. "And you run the orchards by yourself."

Elizabeth lifted her chin. "I do, milady. And still running it at a profit."

Evie smiled at her. "I have no doubt you are. Everything looks perfect." Evie set the photograph down. "Do you keep in contact with your grandfather?"

Elizabeth employed a tone that spoke of defiance when she said, "We correspond."

She wondered if barriers had been set in place to deal with the fact the Baron's daughter had married beneath her.

"My mother married for love," Elizabeth said, almost as if she had read Evie's thoughts.

"I have no doubt she did." Taking her seat, she asked, "How do you get on with the agent, Mr.

Gregory Wellington?"

"Well enough."

"If you have any issues, feel free to come straight to me." Since being rushed through the tour of the tenant farms, Evie had felt Mr. Gregory didn't really care for female interference.

"I couldn't help noticing the proximity to Hollyhock Farm." Evie looked at Tom only to wonder why she had looked at him. Did she need to gain some sort of assurance from him? Regardless, it felt rather good to see him give her a small nod of encouragement. "Living so close, you would get to see the type of people who visit him. You might even hear some of the conversations."

Elizabeth gave her a wary look. "What exactly is it you are asking, my lady?"

She'd slipped. Why had she pretended to be less than she was by referring to her as milady? Did she have issues with being of noble birth? Although, some people would argue against her right to be considered as such because only her mother had been of noble birth.

None of it mattered to Evie but…

Elizabeth might have other ideas if she'd set her cap at someone who might feel inferior to her.

Elizabeth lifted her chin. "I know you haven't actually asked me anything yet, but you are trying to lead up to it."

Oh, yes. Elizabeth Young could look after herself.

"I would like to know if you've heard any conversations that might be deemed disconcerting."

Without hesitating, the young woman asked, "Such as arguing?"

"Yes."

Elizabeth gave her a knowing smile. "No one seems to argue over Charlie Timms' stud fees but they do argue when they can't actually get the service."

The remark took Evie by surprise. Glancing at Tom, she saw the same reaction reflected in his eyes. She had no doubt they were both impressed by Elizabeth Young's astute manner.

Had Elizabeth heard Charlie arguing with Mrs. Howard-Smith because he wanted to end their affair?

"Out of curiosity, do you garden?" Evie asked.

"Not really. I look after a few rose bushes my mother planted. Charlie Timms gives me horse manure because he says roses love it. He knows his plants."

"Do you know if he grows foxglove?"

Elizabeth Young didn't even think about it. "Not since the order came from the house to stop growing it when Lady Woodridge's dog died of poison, or so I'm told. I think I might have only just been born when it happened."

No one grew foxgloves?

They would have to find another poisonous plant…

Evie reminded Elizabeth to never hesitate to ask for help and, thanking her for the tea, left.

On the way back to the car, Tom asked, "That's it? You don't want to talk to Charlie Timms?"

One more day, Evie thought. "Do you know what I think?"

"Do I get three guesses or are you going to tell me?"

Evie tapped her chin in thought. What if Tom got it right the first time? "I'll tell you because I want to continue to believe I am not transparent." She smiled. "I wouldn't want to be so dull. Anyhow, I think Elizabeth Young is keen on Charlie Timms."

Tom looked at her for a long moment. Evie tried to imagine what he might be thinking but her mind failed to yield any suggestions.

"Does that mean she's just become a suspect? After all, she'd want to get rid of her competition."

"No, I don't think so," Evie mused. "In fact, I think Elizabeth is prepared to wait it out." At least now they had confirmation Charlie Timms had tried to end the affair.

Then again…

Could Elizabeth Young be so infatuated she would do and say anything for Charlie Timms?

20

After their visit to Elizabeth Young, they drove straight to the pub so Tom could change out of his black suit. While eager to do the same, Evie suggested stopping by Mrs. Baker's Delights first for an early luncheon.

"Since we were supposed to have gone on to Witford Hall, we won't be expected back until later for a late luncheon. I'm afraid I cannot wait. Also, their game pie is scrumptious."

As they strode in, the young waitress looked up from behind the counter.

Hoping to find the table by the window available, Evie glanced away. When she turned back to the young woman, Evie found her still staring at her, her expression showing a hint of surprise.

Surprised to see Evie at the tea room so soon after the funeral service?

"Table for two?" the young woman asked.

"Yes, please."

Taking her seat, Evie smiled at the waitress

and only then noticed her name embroidered on her apron. "Florence, we would love some of your delectable game pie, please. I've been craving it since I last had it here."

"Thank you for saying so, milady. I'm hoping it will do well in the pie competition at the upcoming fair. Some of our customers have been purchasing them to take home with them and I have even started a delivery service to some locals."

"Well, I would love to have a daily delivery of them but I am afraid my cook might take exception, so I shall have to indulge in secret."

Evie waited for Florence to stride off before saying, "I would hate to get on the wrong side of my cook. Who knows what she might do. I hope word doesn't reach her about me enjoying these pies so much."

Tom laughed. "You are living in fear in your own home?"

"I've only now become aware of how sensitive some people can be." She brushed her finger along the hemline of her dress. "There is nothing wrong with taking precautions and treading with care."

Tom teased, "Not too much care, I hope. Otherwise, you will be doing me out of a job."

Looking out the window, Evie noticed a few villagers dressed in black and wondered if they had attended the funeral. It seemed strange since Mrs. Howard-Smith hadn't really been a local.

"Did we get around to suspecting Everett Townsend? Perhaps we should. He has a greenhouse and his estate doesn't fall under our jurisdiction so it wouldn't be affected by the dowager's edict."

Florence set the plates down. "Enjoy."

The aroma made Evie forget what she'd been talking about.

"It looks good, it smells good," Tom declared. Taking a bite, he added, "And it tastes good."

"This is rather pretty. I didn't notice the crust has Mrs. Baker's Delights pressed into it." That's all she managed to say before falling into silent appreciation of the pie. Several bites later, she looked up and found Tom in a similar state of blissful oblivion.

"Just as good as you suggested," he said.

When Florence strode by their table, Evie said, "Our compliments to the cook."

"Oh, thank you. That'll be me."

"Really? You must be run off your feet."

"I will be getting help now. Since opening the tea room a few months ago, business has been good enough for me to employ someone." Seeing more customers coming in, Florence excused herself.

Devoting all their attention to their meal, Evie waited until they'd finished to say, "It's wonderfully enterprising for someone so young."

"All I can say is we're lucky she set up her tea

room here. This is probably the best pie I have ever had," Tom declared.

On their return to Halton House, Evie mused, "I didn't realize Henrietta could be so dictatorial. Then again, she must have been heartbroken over the loss of her dog. I think I would be too. But would I take such extreme measures and expect everyone to stop growing foxglove?" After a moment of silence, Evie turned to look at Tom.

"Oh, I beg your pardon," he said. "Did you expect me to answer?"

"No, not really." They had fixated on the plant after the detective's odd question about gardening and only because they had come across a book on poisonous plants and then George Mills had told them he didn't grow it on the estate.

Foxglove had seemed to fit the bill. If not foxglove, then which other plant might have been used by the killer? The doctor had initially determined Mrs. Howard-Smith had died of a heart attack, but his findings had clearly been overturned…

As they were not privy to that information, they would have to make do with more guesswork.

"I fear we might be wrong about foxglove being the killer's choice of poison," Evie mused.

"Do you have an alternative in mind?"

"No. We shall have to consult the book of

poisonous plants again. I've been trying to remember why we settled on foxglove?"

Tom brushed his hand across the steering wheel. "We were looking for a garden plant and that one seemed to match the criteria."

"I just had the same thought. Well, we got it wrong."

Tom prompted, "Because…"

"Because no one seems to grow it." Evie clasped her hands and twiddled her thumbs. "Now I'm thinking I've been rather hasty in my conclusion. We know it's not grown on the estate or any of the surrounding farms but perhaps someone in the village grows it." Or someone with an estate nearby like Everett Townsend.

Slowing down, Tom turned and gave her a surprised look. "Are you about to suggest we inspect every garden in the district?"

"I'm sure the police have already done that. Do you think the detective has searched the grounds without asking for permission? I noticed he hasn't returned to make further inquiries or accusations."

This time, Tom laughed. "In your place, I would be relieved."

"Yes, but it means we no longer have the opportunity to prod for information. I wonder why he attended the service?" Unlike Everett Townsend, the detective had made no effort to engage her in conversation.

"To pay his respects?"

Evie twitched her nose.

"Fine. For the same reasons we all did. Curiosity," Tom suggested.

"I am not convinced. He must have had his eye on someone or he might have been waiting for someone to show up. Do you think he's onto Charlie Timms? He's the only person who is somehow involved in all this and who didn't show up at the funeral." She wondered why he had chosen to stay away. Especially after showing so much concern for Mrs. Howard-Smith's reputation. Did he think his presence might have drawn attention to himself and raised questions?

"How do you know he didn't attend?" Tom asked. "He might have been in disguise or he might have stayed well out of sight, maintaining a safe distance. Remember, he doesn't want the affairs to be brought out into the open. His presence might have piqued someone's curiosity."

"Yes. Yes. I believe you have made your point."

"Then again, he might have conned us into believing he was only concerned about the victims' welfare and reputations."

Evie gave a woeful sigh. "Why must people be so underhanded and complicated?"

This produced another laugh from Tom. "I'm surprised you haven't pointed the finger of suspicion at Everett Townsend. He has a greenhouse."

Evie grinned. "I have mentioned him and… We'll get to him in good time."

As they drove through the Halton House gatehouse, Evie leaned forward. "Is that the detective's vehicle?" Evie exclaimed pushing the words out. "I swear my heart is thumping all the way to my throat, if that is at all possible."

Had someone else died?

Tom glanced at her. "Perhaps the detective has come to his senses and has decided to share vital information with you."

"When did you decide to have fun at my expense?"

He laughed. "When I realized you were providing the entertainment without any encouragement whatsoever. Would you like me to turn the motor car around?"

Evie looked over her shoulder at the road behind them. "You have no idea how tempted I am. Do you think he would give chase?"

"There's only one way to find out."

"Aha! Now you're taunting me into providing entertainment. Drive on, please. I wish to hear what the detective has to say."

"Yes, ma'am."

They pulled up outside the front steps just as Edgar opened the front door. Evie frowned. "He took his time."

"You're right. When we arrive, Edgar opens the door immediately. He must have seen us approaching and decided to wait for us to arrive. You obviously take precedence over the detective who is clearly fuming."

Yes, she could see that. Detective Inspector O'Neill stood on the doorstep tapping his foot and slapping one hand against the other.

"Good morning," Evie greeted him. "What brings you out this way, detective?"

"Lady Woodridge." He tipped his hat. "I had intended approaching you at the service, but then decided against it. Too many eyes and ears," he explained.

"How considerate. Do come in. I will ring for some tea. That is, if you're brave enough to have some."

"It would be most welcomed. Thank you."

She led him through to the library. Glancing over her shoulder, she saw Tom following them several steps behind.

"By the way, detective. Have you heard of anyone who has a litter of puppies?"

He looked somewhat confused.

"I'm looking to adopt one." Despite Caro's objections, Evie wanted to spread the word around about her interest in a puppy. The sooner Caro got used to the idea, the sooner she would stop sabotaging Evie's clothes…

"No, I'm sorry, I haven't."

"Strange. I would have expected spring to be the perfect time for an abundance of new litters." Turning to Edgar, she asked for some tea and cake to be brought in. "Are you, by any chance, here to take a sample of my special blend of tea? I noticed you didn't take any last time you were here. I don't wish to be granted special privileges. In fact, I should insist you take some. Although, it should be enough if you drink some."

For the first time, the detective looked uncomfortable.

If Henrietta had overheard her, she would have given her a warning to behave. Instead, she had to suffer Tom's roll of the eyes.

"I noticed you at the service today, inspector. Did your suspect turn up?"

"There appears to be a conspiracy of silence," he said. "I have been trying to find out where the victims dined on the night of their deaths but no one has come forward with the information." He shook his head. "It strikes me as odd that no one should have seen them on their final night until they both arrived home late in the evening."

The detective looked at Evie long and hard.

At first, she held still. So still, she held her breath. Evie smiled and shifted. She hoped those were not the signs of a guilty mind. "I can confirm I had dinner with several people on the night of Mrs. Hallesberry's death. As for the night of the first victim's death… I'm afraid I retired early and you only have my word for it."

"I don't mean to suggest you are still under suspicion." He held his hands out, palms up.

"See, I don't even have my notebook out."

So… She had been held under suspicion.

Regardless, why had the detective decided to pay her another visit? Surely, he didn't really think she could help him.

Evie curled her fingers around the armrests. She had been keeping vital information from him and she had to snatch this opportunity and come clean. Yes, she needed to rid her conscience of guilt before it became an issue. She simply couldn't see a way around it. She would have to name Charlie Timms.

The detective leaned back in his chair and drummed his fingers on the armrest. "What astonishes me is that an entire village knew about Dr. Browning driving out in the middle of the night, but no one saw either of the ladies' cars on the road. It makes one wonder if they are all hiding something… or trying to protect someone."

Evie shared a look with Tom as she silently congratulated herself for reaching that conclusion all by herself.

If, as the detective claimed, everyone knew about the doctor's emergency house call, did they also know about Charlie Timms?

She had witnessed the committee ladies' reaction to Charlie and that could not have been the first time it had happened.

What would compel everyone to maintain their silence and unite in solidarity? She imagined local men aspiring to be like him and local women entertaining dreams of being with him.

"I'm afraid I can't help you, detective. Despite being within walking distance of the village, we are rather sheltered from all noise here." Including gossip; something she thought she had covered with Caro acting as her go-between.

Tom cleared his throat.

Instead of looking at him, Evie dropped her eyes to her hands and inspected her nails.

"Do you know what strikes me as odd, detective?" she asked.

"What's that, my lady?"

"We live in one of the prettiest villages in Berkshire, with award winning gardens and yet no one plants foxglove. It's almost a quintessential cottage garden plant, but no one cultivates it. Mr. Winchester and I had developed a theory about the plant. However, now we have doubts."

"There are other poisonous plants besides that one." Detective Inspector O'Neill stopped himself from saying more by changing the subject. "There is one key person missing from the timeline of events."

Edgar walked in carrying the tea tray.

"I think once word spreads about your search, someone will come forward." In the meantime, she would pay Charlie Timms one final visit and ask him to provide the exact times his lovers had visited.

Tom shifted and, in the process, he drew Evie's attention to him in time to see his lifted eyebrow. Had he read her mind? Did he mean to prompt her into naming Charlie Timms?

Accepting a cup of tea, the detective took one sip and set the cup down. "There is one more thing. I hesitate to mention it but I fear I must. The committee ladies have expressed concerns about you. I have tried to dissuade them from believing they are in any danger from you, all to no avail. I'm afraid they have asked that you stay away from them."

Evie's lips parted but she failed to find the right words to convey her shock.

She had been labeled a threat?

21

Led down the garden path

"I almost felt sorry for the detective. He looked tired. Did you notice? He has a hard task ahead of him and, while I don't mean to be harsh, it's his job to wade through the list of suspects."

Tom slipped his hands inside his pockets and whistled a tune under his breath.

"Is there something you wish to say?" Evie asked.

"Are you trying to justify your decision to withhold information from him?"

"There's no need to do that. I've already explained. There are enough people spreading rumors around. I should like to get my facts straight before making any statements to the police. Besides, it's his job to round up suspects. Who am I to interfere?" She waited to see if she could get away with the remark or if Tom would remind her how much prodding she had done only recently.

"What if his entire investigation hinges on

talking with Charlie Timms?" When she didn't answer, Tom shrugged. "You've done this before."

"What?"

"Bided your time. Waited for the right moment to share information and it nearly got the Duke of Heatherington killed."

Evie groaned. Recently, she had delayed passing on some vital information to her friend, Bicky, the Duke of Heatherington, and he had ended up being shot. That time, she had been concerned about breeching protocols. One simply did not barge into a duke's home and burst into a bout of hysterics over an incident that might not even have been an incident.

Evie surged to her feet. "If we were led to Charlie Timms, then the inspector should eventually find his way to him."

"Where are we going?" Tom asked as he followed Evie out of the library.

"To speak with Charlie Timms again. In fact, before this day is out, I will have spoken with everyone I crossed paths with since my arrival. Meaning, I will leave no stone unturned."

"Remind me again why you are getting involved?"

Striding out into the patio, Evie wondered why she hadn't gone out through the front door. Now they would have to walk the long way around. "Actually, I have a better idea." Realizing she hadn't answered his question, she said, "Because I seem to have more time on my hands than I know what to do with." If Henrietta had been within hearing, she might have suggested rolling up her sleeves and working out the details for the Hunt Ball.

"In other words, you are bored."

Yes, Evie thought.

The condition appeared to have crept up on her.

"I think you're headed the wrong way."

"No, I'm not. This is about my bright idea." They walked along the path leading to the stables and the garden shed next to it where they found the gardener, George Mills, filling a wheelbarrow with hay.

"How can I help you, milady?"

"We would like to tap into your expertise, George. We now know foxglove is rather dangerous. What other plants might be considered equally fatal?" And did they grow any on the estate? She didn't ask the question because she assumed it would be a resounding no.

George raked his fingers through his hair. "There are quite a few, milady." He looked around him. Either because he wanted to find inspiration or because he wished to get away from Evie.

"That's fine, George. Don't worry if you can't think of the names."

"It's not that, milady. There is a book but I

don't have it in my possession. Someone borrowed it and hasn't returned it."

"Who might that be? Perhaps they might allow us to have a look at it."

"Charlie Timms."

***

"Now will you contact the detective and tell him what you know about Charlie Timms?"

"What? Before getting the book? Don't be silly." Evie hurried her pace toward the roadster. "Make haste. We don't want him to poison someone else… And, no, I am not accusing him of being the poisoner."

She heard Tom murmur something under his breath but could not make it out. "Are you, by any chance, complaining? Considering how much trouble has resulted from people expressing their dissent, I would advise against giving any contradictory opinions. We must work as a team, or not at all. Do you think you can get into the spirit of it?"

Tom gave her a tight smile. "Are you asking me to forego all personal opinions and become your cheering squad? Rah, rah, rah?"

Evie laughed. "Nonsense. You are allowed to have opinions. Only, try to cultivate the same opinions I hold."

He held the passenger door open for her. "You said that with a serious face."

Pressing her lips together, Evie held on to her serious look for as long as she could.

"I feel we need to change the subject," Evie suggested.

They made their way to Hollyhock Farm chatting about the pretty views and revisiting the subject of appropriate dog breeds.

"Before you even suggest it, I should like to state I am in no way inclined to believe Charlie Timms is a poisoner. The fact he has a book which might have assisted him means nothing. I have books on the subject and you don't see me cavorting around the county killing people."

Tom looked about ready to say something but appeared to change his mind.

"Let me guess, you were about to say I have been supplied with more than enough reasons to exact my revenge on a certain group of ladies." When Tom didn't answer, Evie added, "The less you say, the more inclined I am to believe you have something to say."

"This might sound like an afterthought, but as the saying goes, better late than never… Remind me never to argue with you. I fear it might be a losing battle."

Evie checked her watch. "I should have told Edgar we were leaving. Now, I'm afraid we'll have to hurry back or risk disappointing the cook by being late to luncheon. Now that I think about it, I hope we don't arrive at an inopportune time. I wouldn't want to interrupt Charlie's lunch."

When Charlie Timms answered the door, a serviette in hand and a miniscule piece of crust on the edge of his lip, Evie apologized. "I am so sorry. We seem to have caught you right in the middle of lunch."

"How can I help you, milady?"

Evie experienced a moment of doubt. Her confidence dwindled and then took a dive. Asking for the book would mean bringing them both face to face with the dangerous subject.

What if she had misjudged him? What if she had been wrong to give him the benefit of the doubt? What if he reacted by brandishing a revolver?

Numerous possibilities paraded through her mind.

Tom stepped forward. "Lady Woodridge is in the process of acquiring a puppy and she has heard of the embargo on a certain plant put in place by the dowager. We understand there is a book identifying all poisonous plants…"

Tom didn't need to explain himself further.

Charlie Timms gave a brisk nod. "Aye. I still remember the episode. I must have been a lad when that happened." He gave another nod. "I know the book you mean. I borrowed it a while back when I decided to establish the stud farm." He stepped back and waved them in. "I'll fetch it for you."

Tom pressed his hand against the small of Evie's back and gently encouraged her in.

It took some doing to get her legs to work. Evie whispered, "I worked myself into a corner just then, entertaining worst case scenarios."

She glanced around the tidy parlor and noticed a tray on a small table. She felt dreadful for interrupting his midday meal. Taking a small step, she inspected the plate and saw that he'd been enjoying a pie.

"Here we are."

"Oh, thank you and I'm sorry, we appear to have caught you in the middle of lunch. Is that a pie from Mrs. Baker's Delights?"

"Yes, it is, milady. They're a gift sent from heaven. I place an order once a week and they deliver. If more of the village stores could do that, I would be able to add an extra few hours to my week and avoid having to do the purchasing myself. I highly recommend the game pie."

Evie exchanged a look with Tom. "That happens to be our favorite too." Holding up the book, she thanked him. "Oh, before I forget. We wondered… the last time Mrs. Howard-Smith came to visit you, do you happen to remember what time that might have been?"

"Five o'clock, milady. I'd been chatting with Elizabeth Young from next door…"

Thanking him, they left.

"That is way too early. According to the maid, Mrs. Howard-Smith didn't get home until late." Where had she gone? "Just as well I didn't give up Charlie Timms' name. He's off the hook."

Peering at Tom, she prompted, “Is there something you wish to say?”

“I am only wondering why you are so eager to take his word?”

“I had considered the possibility,” she thought out loud. “Yes, he might have a particular character trait. Are you suggesting I have fallen under his spell?” Evie gasped. “You are!”

“You sound offended.”

“With good reason. I have already explained my decision to trust Charlie Timms and it has nothing to do with his good looks or easy manner.”

“Good looks?”

Exasperated by his teasing and the unfair appraisal he had clearly formed in his mind, Evie hurried on head. Even as an impressionable debutante, she had never been one to flutter her eyelashes at handsome gentlemen.

Whistling a popular Al Johnson love song, Tom followed several steps behind.

Evie found herself humming along to the tune. “You made me love you. I didn’t want to do it. I didn’t want to do it… You made me want you. And all the while you knew it…”

Half an hour later, Evie groaned under her breath. They had immersed themselves in the book of poisons. And, despite reading out loud, the tune continued to weave through her mind…

22

"Mr. Everett Townsend sends his apologies. He realizes he might have overreacted and understands you were only making jest of the circumstances to lighten the mood," Henrietta announced when she found Evie and Tom in the dining room. "Ah, I see you are having a late luncheon. Sara went straight to the library to make a telephone call and Phillipa needed to change out of her mourning clothes, but they should be here momentarily."

"Would you care to join us?" Evie invited.

"Oh, yes. I'm rather famished. It's difficult to indulge in sustenance when people around you are in a state of deep sorrow." She glanced down at their plates. "Oh, pie. My favorite."

Evie took a long sip of wine. "Yes, we have had our share of pie today. First at Mrs. Baker's Delights and now here. Mrs. Horace surprised us with game pie." Apparently, Evie's cook had been hearing far too many positive reviews of the new establishment in the village and had decided to outdo Mrs. Baker's Delights by preparing what she considered to be a superior pie.

"And how does it measure up?" Henrietta asked as Sara joined them.

Evie leaned in and whispered, "The crust is not as buttery, otherwise, it's quite good." Raising her tone, she added, "We should have pie at least once a month." She hoped the news would travel down to the kitchen, leaving her with the rest of the month to enjoy her pies in the village.

Sara laughed under her breath. "Honestly, you seem to forget she is working for you."

"I don't wish to hurt her feelings." And, in the process, instigate another offensive attack against her. "By the way, Henrietta, I am so sorry to hear about your puppy."

Henrietta looked taken aback. "My puppy?"

"The one you lost when it ate some foxglove."

Henrietta gave her a sheepish smile. "I've never owned a dog in my life."

"What? But everyone says they've been issued orders to never grow the plant again."

Henrietta made a dismissive gesture with her hand. "I simply wanted those silly plants out of sight. Don't ask me why but I have never liked them. Actually, it might have something to do with my Irish nanny. She would tell me bedtime stories about fairies living inside the little tubes." Henrietta shivered. "She never failed to embellish her tales by describing the fairies as having pointy teeth that would nibble the tip of my nose if I didn't eat all my supper because they would know, oh yes, they would definitely know I had been naughty."

When she finished telling her tale, they all swayed back as if released from a spell.

"How perfectly dreadful." For both young Henrietta and the foxgloves that might have flourished on the estate.

Henrietta brightened. "Oh, I remembered what I meant to tell you when I came in. Everett Townsend has a garden full of foxglove, but they are only now coming through. He says his gardener collects the seeds and grows seedlings."

"We can hardly include him as a suspect," Evie reasoned. "What possible motive would he have?"

"To whom are you referring? Everett or his gardener?"

"Both, I suppose. Did he give a reason for eavesdropping on the committee ladies?"

"He did. He says women don't realize men are always at a disadvantage because they miss out on gossip."

"What nonsense," Sara said. "Men have their sewing circles too. Not that they would ever admit it."

They all looked at Tom.

"I shall take the road of least resistance and agree with everyone's opinions."

"How marvelous," Henrietta exclaimed. "We have only known him a short time and we have already trained him into compliance."

Evie begged to differ. When had her destiny changed to include an entourage of people who disagreed with her?

Phillipa strode in. "Oh, how dreadful it is to have to wear black to funerals. I am so glad to be out of those clothes."

Evie gestured to Edgar who immediately organized another place setting at the table.

Henrietta cleared her throat. "Now that we are all here…"

Evie's shoulders slumped. "Are you about to deliver bad news? I'm not sure I can take any more." If Henrietta could issue an edict banning the cultivation of a plant, then… Evie felt she ought to be able to insist no bad news be shared by anyone within her household. Realizing that would take far too much effort, she abandoned the idea.

"Don't be such a killjoy, Evangeline. I merely wanted to share a message passed on to me by Mrs. Penn."

"Your spy?"

"Yes. She tells me their determination is beginning to dwindle."

"Does that even matter? I thought we had already agreed they no longer have a leg to stand on."

"I am surprised at you, Evangeline. At the start, you appeared to support an amicable resolution. Now you seem to want to rub our imminent victory in their faces."

Why did she feel everyone had decided to conspire against her and pretend to be in opposition to everything she did and said?

"Did you end up sending the invitations?" Evie asked.

"Yes, of course. The show must go on."

"Do I have a role to play? I should like to be involved."

"But I thought you were busy playing 'Keystone Cops' with Tom, chasing down the killer? And, according to Edgar, the detective is now consulting with you."

"I wouldn't go so far as to say that." Evie tapped her chin. She and Tom had been pouring through the book of poisonous plants they had procured from Charlie Timms and hadn't given any thought to anything else.

If Mrs. Howard-Smith had gone to see Charlie late in the afternoon, where else did she go afterwards?

She would have been devastated by Charlie Timms' insistence they end the affair. Did she seek the company of a friendly ear, someone she could confide in?

Someone who endcd up being the wrong person…

Sitting up, Evie realized she might have found yet another missing link. This probably put her two more steps ahead of the detective.

"I wonder how one becomes a detective."

23

"I hear the Hunt Ball is to go ahead, milady."

Caro's remark took Evie by surprise, so much so, she missed a step as she strode into her bedroom. Had Caro changed tactics? Or had she escalated her efforts to express her displeasure over Evie's decisions? Would she now wait to catch her by surprise? She could almost sympathize with the committee ladies and their growing concerns about being targets.

"Yes. Full steam ahead." Did Caro have a problem with that?

"I'm ever so glad to hear that, milady. This house needs a cheerful event. There has already been too much gloom and doom."

Too true, Evie agreed and wondered if Caro's remarks were meant to be a lead up to her renewed efforts to have Seth Halton living here, filling the house with laughter.

Evie decided to try a tactic of her own, using diversion to steer her maid away from pursuing whatever plot she had contrived. "Caro?"

"Yes, milady."

"If you suffered from a broken heart, would you seek the company of a friend?"

"Of course. Usually, I have a chat with Mrs. Arnold. Despite never marrying, she's very understanding and knows what to say."

Yes, Evie had always had that impression about the housekeeper. "Does she listen to everyone's problems?"

"She does. She encourages all the maids to talk through any problem they might have with her. She says it avoids confusion and complications. A problem shared is a problem halved."

Evie waited for Caro to mention anyone else. Would Caro confide in her? Indeed, had she ever come to her with personal concerns? Evie felt she could tell her maid anything and know it wouldn't go any further…

"And, of course, you know I would always ask for your advice."

Evie brightened. "Oh, I'm glad to hear you say so."

She couldn't picture Mrs. Howard-Smith running to anyone for help. Not even the committcc ladies who all obviously knew about the amorous shenanigans going on. Had they all been in on the secret? Had they all known about it without bringing it out into the open?

"You look preoccupied, milady."

Slipping off her shoes, Evie sat down and

smiled. "I'm pushing myself for answers to no avail. Tell me about your new dress. Did you find something you liked?"

She listened to Caro talk at length about the new fashions and how they didn't feel quite right on her. This provided Evie with something to take her mind off the many unanswered questions filling her head. Unfortunately, it didn't last. The dinner table and after dinner conversations focused on recent events and the moment her head hit the pillow, thoughts about everything that had been happening cropped up and flourished in her mind, staying there during most of the night.

***

"I will be sorry to miss the ball, but I'm sure my motor car will have been fixed by then. How many guests have been invited?" Phillipa asked during breakfast.

"Henrietta probably extended invitations to fifty people. This isn't London and as we could only really accommodate half of those people for overnight stays, she would have limited herself to those living nearby."

Phillipa's slightly glazed eyes suggested Evie had provided more information than she had expected.

"The ballroom is large," Evie continued, "but hardly the size of Mrs. Astor's. Even so, we don't want to squash people in."

"Mrs. Astor? Who is she?" Phillipa laughed. "Sorry, I just heard myself. I'm sure I'm supposed to know the name."

"The Astor family is quite prominent in New York. Mrs. Astor could only fit four hundred into her ballroom so she limited her invitations to only the most elite. Over the years, it became quite the thing to refer to the four hundred. I'm not even sure they still entertain as much since the matriarch of the family died."

"Does your family belong to the four hundred?"

Tilting her head in thought, Evie smiled. "I believe my mother attended a soiree held by Mrs. Astor but she found the woman too snooty and that's saying something considering how snooty my mother can be. I believe she feels she has made the ultimate statement by having her daughter marry into British aristocracy. I suppose that makes me her sacrificial lamb. Just as well I married for love."

"Do you have any idea how unusual that is?"

Nodding, Evie helped herself to more bacon. "I have been rather lucky." Up to a point, she thought. Although, this new phase of her life appeared to be looking up.

Speaking of which, Evie's gaze slid over to the door. "I'm surprised Tom hasn't made an appearance."

"Perhaps he's canvassing the village,"

Phillipa suggested.

Evie set her fork down. Without her? "Did he mention something?"

"No, but he looks like a man of action. I wouldn't be surprised if he takes matters into his own hands. Although, he seems to rather enjoy working with you."

"Working? That's rather an odd way of putting it."

"How would you describe what you have been doing together?"

Evie arranged some scrambled eggs onto her fork. "We are collaborating on a puzzle but only because I have been dragged into it by groundless accusations. Otherwise, I can assure you, I would keep my nose right out of it."

Edgar refilled her cup and she looked up in time to see a raised eyebrow.

"Edgar? Do you disagree?"

"I don't believe it is my place to hold an opinion, my lady."

"What nonsense. Out with it," Evie encouraged.

Edgar straightened and gave her a most imperious look. "I suppose I believe you have a certain advantage over the detective. You are welcomed as a social equal in places where he will always be considered an outsider."

Surprised by his response, Evie brightened. "I believe you are encouraging me, Edgar. Thank you."

He inclined his head slightly and resumed his post by the buffet table.

"I only wish Tom had been here to listen to your fine testimonial."

At the sound of someone clearing their throat, Evie turned. "Oh, I spoke too soon. Did you catch any of that, Tom?"

Adjusting his tie, he made his way to the buffet table and helped himself to breakfast.

"Yes, do join us for breakfast," Evie teased when in actual fact she rather enjoyed seeing him make himself at home.

"Edgar does have a point," Tom said. "You can move about with far more freedom than the detective. Yet, you seem to be restraining yourself."

"Oh? What am I missing?"

"You haven't made any efforts to speak with Dr. Browning's maid and she seems to be a source of information."

True. However, Mrs. Browning remained at the center of the original debacle and Evie did not feel inclined to grace her doorstep with her presence. "It would have to be a clandestine meeting." She stared at the landscape beyond the window. "Oh, I've got it. We even have an enticing carrot. We can use Henrietta's butler to lure the maid. We should organize that today. And while we're in the village, we might drop in on Mrs. Baker's Delights and try one of her other pies. We must support local businesses."

The edge of Tom's lip lifted.

"I believe Tom wishes to say I have just justified paying the local establishment another visit when, in reality, I wish to eat another one of their scrumptious pies."

"Well?" Phillipa asked. "Did the Countess get it right?"

"I wouldn't dare contradict my hostess," Tom said. "I'm sure I would have formed the same opinion. However, I had been busy thinking how good these sausages look. Pity I shall have to leave room for the pies."

24

"It's a fine day for a stroll and a good way to ensure we have enough room for the pies." In reality, Evie had suggested walking to the village so Phillipa could come along with them. The roadster could only really accommodate two people and that meant leaving her out of their adventures and missing out on her valuable input.

"You must feel like a princess, coming down from her tower to mingle with her people," Phillipa mused. "Do the local villagers bow and curtsey?"

"I don't expect them to. The ones I come into contact with are quite polite. That's enough for me." Slipping her hands inside her coat pockets, her fingers collided with the envelope she had been transferring from pocket to pocket every day. Evie glanced over at Tom and decided to once again postpone discussing the contents of her telegram.

"I have been meaning to ask you if you could have a talk with my maid, Caro. She had trouble finding a new dress and I believe she is lacking confidence."

Phillipa chuckled. "I'm not sure I'm the person to inspire her. Most people find this new fashion rather daring and outrageous."

"I think you look smashing in your trousers." The colorful ensemble included tangerine orange with white stripes trousers and a white jacket. "I don't mean to be intrusive and just ignore me if I am, but how did you manage to make your way to England?" She had mentioned her parents owned a cattle ranch, so Evie assumed they had funded her trip.

Phillipa gave her a sheepish smile. "A tiny inheritance from a spinster aunt. I seem to have a few of those. I wonder if that bodes well for me? Spinsterhood seems to run in my family. Anyhow, I'm hoping to eventually make my own way through my writing but first I must gain some sort of life experience."

"You've landed in the right place," Tom murmured. "Have you considered writing mysteries? Or perhaps Lady Woodridge can engage your services to document her adventures."

Evie nudged Phillipa. "He is poking fun at me."

"I am not," he assured her.

"You make me sound like a swashbuckling buccaneer and I am nothing of the sort."

Arriving at the village green, they stopped to

appreciate the blooms, spending a few moments of quiet reflection at the monument which had been erected to honor the fallen. The little village was alive with activity with the locals going about their business.

"The dower house is up ahead. We should find Henrietta attending to her morning correspondence. I'm sure she won't mind our impromptu visit."

"I shouldn't think so," Phillipa piped in. "Considering how she drops in on you all the time. Anyone would think she is keeping tabs on you."

"She means well. Now, I need to remember her butler's name."

"I've heard her mention her chauffeur, Hobson. But I'm afraid I can't help with the butler." Phillipa laughed. "Although, I am keen to meet him. He seems to have quite a following."

Evie thought about bees buzzing around a flower. That led her to think about the possibility of a third woman having an affair with Charlie Timms. A woman who then decided she didn't wish to share him with anyone else. She had already considered the possibility but had found it too ludicrous to pursue. Something she now found odd. If two women had been prepared to risk everything and act on their fantasies then she couldn't see any reason why there couldn't be a third one.

She had a good mind to follow Mrs. Browning to see how she spent her days. Smiling to herself, Evie looked toward the village. Her smile wavered. “Is that the detective’s car?”

“Where?” Tom asked.

“At the end of the street. He’s looking away now but a second ago, I would swear he’d been keeping an eye out for someone.”

They hurried past the gated entrance and along the path decorated with large earthenware urns heavy with colorful springtime blooms. The garden paid homage to the season with bursts of color and decorative trees including maples and oranges with a few fruit still on the trees.

At the door, Tom pulled on the bell. When the butler answered the door, Tom introduced himself. “And you must be the butler.”

“Bradley.”

Evie sidled up to Tom. Oh, yes. She could see why the doctor’s maid had fallen for the butler. Tall with broad shoulders, he had an easy smile and eyes that sparkled with hidden amusement. Unlike most butlers she’d met, he couldn’t be older than thirty.

“Hello, Bradley. Is the dowager receiving visitors this morning?”

“I shall announce you, my lady.” He gestured for them to follow him.

Evie felt like a giddy debutante, awestruck by the sight of a good-looking man. Phillipa nudged her and giggled as she murmured,

"Scrumptious."

Trust Henrietta to hire a handsome butler.

"Evangeline." Henrietta set her fountain pen down and rose to her feet. "What a pleasant surprise. Bradley. Please bring some tea."

Evie took a seat near Henrietta's desk. "Oh, my goodness. You have an uninterrupted view of the village."

"Oh, yes. Now that you mention it. I rarely notice these days. Although, I had to have the hedge trimmed as it had been growing out of control and blocking my view of the vicarage."

And they couldn't have that…

"Have you come to once again extend your generous invitation to return to Halton House?"

Evie could see she would have to beg. Instead of playing into the dowager's hands, she chose to draw out the game. Shifting to the edge of her chair, Evie said, "Henrietta. We need your butler to lure the doctor's maid here."

"Your choice of words suggests this should be done by stealth."

Evie gave a vigorous nod. "Yes, the less people who know about it, the better. Is there some way she can come in through the back? I noticed the detective out on the road and I wouldn't want him to know what I'm up to."

"I shall instruct Bradley to take the lane. It should give him some alone time with the maid. He'll either appreciate it or curse me for it. But what is this all about?"

In all truth, Evie couldn't remember. "Some tea first, please. The walk made me thirsty." She glanced at Phillipa and tried to recall what they had been discussing at breakfast. "Oh, yes!" she exclaimed.

Henrietta looked at her as if she had just grown an extra head. "Are you quite right there, my dear?"

"We need to know where Mrs. Howard-Smith went after…" Evie frowned and tried to remember if she had told Henrietta about the affair with Charlie Timms.

"After?" Henrietta prompted.

"After her visit with Charlie Timms. He says she stopped by at five in the afternoon."

"Stopped by, did she?" Henrietta shook her head. "I just had an image I know nanny would have heartily disapproved of."

"If it helps any, they argued because Charlie Timms told her he wanted to end the affair."

"And what does all this have to do with the doctor's maid?"

"I have a theory. I think Mrs. Howard-Smith might have sought out a friend or someone to lend her an ear."

"And you think that person might have been the doctor's wife."

"Yes."

When Bradley brought in the tea, Henrietta took him aside and explained what they wanted. Resuming her seat, Henrietta nodded. "He pretends to be reserved but I suspect he harbors a secret identity which yearns for excitement. You might just have provided the key to unlock this. Although, I don't know what will come of it. I only hope I don't lose my butler over this. I shall hold you responsible if I do."

Tom moved toward a window and peered out. Had the detective been waiting for them to appear? How would he have known they would be coming to the village? What if the detective wanted to keep an eye on Henrietta? Evie suggested Tom find a room upstairs where he might gain a better view of the street and report back on the detective's moves.

Henrietta murmured, "This is becoming more intriguing by the minute."

They had nearly finished their tea when the young maid walked into the drawing room, bobbed a curtsey and introduced herself as Pearl, all the while keeping her adoring eyes on the butler who appeared to be struggling to maintain his composure.

"You won't get the doctor or his wife into any sort of trouble," Henrietta assured Pearl. "We only wish to know if Mrs. Howard-Smith visited on the night she died."

Pearl gasped and pressed her hand to her mouth. "Visited? As a ghost?"

Henrietta shook her head in disbelief. "No. No. Before she died."

Relieved, the maid nodded. "Yes. She did."

25

"I don't quite understand," Henrietta exclaimed. "Have you made progress or not?"

Pearl, the doctor's maid, had confirmed Evie's suspicions. Mrs. Howard-Smith had visited Mrs. Browning.

But they had then left together.

Where had they gone?

"We do know more than we did a while ago."

"I would be incredibly disappointed if you didn't, Evangeline. As the Countess of Woodridge, you need to set a fine example. People are watching and some are even waiting for you to flounder."

Really? Evie wanted to remain focused otherwise, she would have asked for more details. If someone wished to see her putting a foot wrong, what did that say about the person and their feelings about her?

Sara came in. Surprised to see them all, she stopped at the door. "If I had known we had visitors, I would have come in. It's such a lovely day and I've been reading the most interesting book… What did I miss?"

"Henrietta will fill you in. I'm afraid we must be going now. We'll see you both at dinner tonight?"

"Oh," Henrietta exchanged a glance with Sara. "That sounds so uncertain."

"Henrietta. Sara. Would you like to join us for dinner tonight?"

The dowagers both nodded. "Oh, how marvelous. Yes, thank you."

They stepped out into the hallway and headed toward the back of the house. Half way along, Evie heard Sara wonder why they were headed out that way.

"She might be right," Phillipa murmured. "Don't you think we'll draw more attention to ourselves? The detective must be waiting for us to emerge from the house. What is he going to think when we don't make an appearance?"

"He will probably tire of waiting long before then. He'll end up thinking we have been invited to stay on for luncheon and move on to spying on someone else." Evie didn't have any room in her head to think about that. "The chauffeur," she whispered.

"What about the chauffeur?" Tom asked.

"You heard me?"

"I have a keen sense of hearing."

They trekked across the back garden and headed toward the gate, walking in single file along the path. "We'll have to go through the paddock."

"Evie?" Tom prompted. "What about the chauffeur?"

"Oh, yes… There is one person who knows where Mrs. Howard-Smith went the night she died. Her chauffeur." And Tom had already spoken with him at the funeral service. So, he shouldn't have any trouble engaging him in conversation.

A minute later, Evie said, "Now that I think about it, this doesn't make sense. Surely the detective talked to him. In which case, he would know exactly how or rather where Mrs. Howard-Smith spent her evening." Evie slowed down. Looking over her shoulder, she saw Tom striding a couple of steps behind, his hands in his pockets, whistling a light tune under his breath as if he didn't have a care in the world.

"Is something wrong?" he asked.

Instead of opening the gate, she waved her hands and urged Tom and Phillipa to turn around. "We must go back out the way we came in."

When Tom widened his eyes in surprise, Phillipa said, "It is a woman's prerogative to change her mind and yours is not to reason why."

Entering the manor house by the back door, they walked along the hallway and as they reached the front of the house, they heard Henrietta and Sara having a quiet conversation.

"Is there a reason why we had to go through the house again?" Tom asked. "We could have gone around…" He shook his head. "Never mind."

"My apologies," Evie offered. "I'm fixated on the task." They encountered the butler who inclined his head and, without asking questions, led the way to the front door.

"Thank you, Bradley." Turning to Tom, she said, "He had no problem with us going through the house." She thought she heard Tom murmur something about aristocrats and eccentricity.

Once outside, Tom asked, "Are we to follow your lead or are you going to fill us in on your plan?"

"There's no plan," Evie admitted. "Not really. I just think it's about time I come clean and share some information with the detective."

They found him still standing by his car. Seeing them, he brushed his mouth with a serviette. That's when Evie realized he'd been eating something.

"Hello, detective. Fancy meeting you here. I see you're eating al fresco." Taking a look at what he held, she exclaimed, "Oh, a pie. Is it one from Mrs. Baker's Delights?"

"It most certainly is. Chicken and quite tasty too."

The detective's friendly tone caught Evie off guard. Had he decided to soften his approach to honey sweetness in order to win Evie's co-operation? It could certainly work both ways. "Tom and I highly recommend the game pie. In fact, we were on our way over to get some. Would you care to join us?"

"Yes, thank you. I only hope I can keep this from my wife. I would get an earful if she finds out I have had more than my fair share."

Convinced the detective had changed tactics and now wanted a friendlier approach, Evie set her mind to getting a fair exchange of information.

At Mrs. Baker's Delights, the waitress, Florence, showed them through to a table and handed them a menu each.

As Evie studied the list, she smacked her lips. "I'm really trying to stick to my purpose and select something different, but my taste buds are clamoring for another game pie."

"I've heard so much about it," Phillipa said, "I'm not even bothering to look at the menu."

"How is your investigation progressing, detective?"

"Not as smoothly as I would wish. I'm beginning to think everyone is intent on safeguarding a secret almost as if they have far too much to lose."

Florence approached them and took their orders.

"I suppose Mrs. Howard-Smith's chauffeur couldn't provide much information."

The detective looked up and met her gaze.

Evie had been brought up to appreciate and practice the art of conversation, engaging people with light but witty dialogue. She managed well enough, but she knew she didn't have what it took to be truly invasive.

Personally, she had never enjoyed pushing for more than a person had been willing to reveal. Of course, that never stopped other people from putting her in the line of fire and wearing her out with incessant questions about her life as if a single secret about her could empower them with some sort of ownership over her.

"We have spoken with the chauffeur," he revealed. "Mrs. Howard-Smith visited Mrs. Browning in the evening."

"And before that?"

The detective shrugged. "She attended your afternoon tea."

The chauffeur hadn't mentioned her visit to Hollyhock Farm? It took every ounce of control to refrain from sharing a look with Tom. They both now knew the chauffeur had withheld information. Why? Out of loyalty to the victim or the family?

"I assume you have spoken with the doctor's wife."

He nodded.

This time, she couldn't help herself. However, when her gaze strayed to Tom, she made a point of then looking out of the window as if that had been her intention all along. In that brief exchange, they both silently acknowledged the fact they now also knew Mrs. Browning had lied to the police. Or rather, she had withheld vital information.

Why would she do that? Especially if she also feared she might be the next victim. Wouldn't she want the culprit captured before he got to her?

Someone nudged her foot. Glancing from one person to the other, she got a nod from Tom who then nudged his head toward the detective.

No. she wouldn't tell him about the doctor's maid. If Mrs. Browning hadn't confided in the detective when he'd questioned her, why would she do so now?

"What about Mrs. Hallesberry? She suffered the same fate." Evie's eyes drew down. Had she also sought out Mrs. Browning for advice?

"We know even less about her whereabouts before returning home. Her chauffeur insists he drove her straight there."

Two chauffeurs withholding information.

"I'm curious." Evie fidgeted with the cutlery. "Why is it so important to find out where the victims went in the evening before returning home?"

Sighing, the detective gave a slow shake of his head.

"You are not at liberty to tell me?" Evie asked.

"Lady Woodridge, I am trying to maintain a sense of professionalism. Please understand, it is highly irregular for a member of the police to… appear to seek the co-operation of a member of the public."

Evie nibbled the edge of her lip as she thought about a recent experience. "I admit to wanting to exchange information but only because we have formed certain theories." She fell silent again and ran through everything she knew. "Your interest in filling a gap suggests you might need to link it to something else."

To his credit, the detective kept his poker face in place.

"What we don't know," Evie said, "is the exact manner of the victims' death. It would help to know which poison is responsible for their deaths. Time plays a factor. We have assumed that much."

Both of Tom's eyebrows hitched up giving Evie the impression she had succeeded in making quite an impression on him.

"They were either killed by a slow working poison or a fast one. Which is it?" She drummed her fingers on the table. When he didn't answer, she leaned forward. "Recently, a close acquaintance succumbed to the effects of poison. I asked the doctor who examined her enough questions to know the victim had been given a small dose of poison, strong enough to kill her but small enough to require several hours to take effect."

The detective brushed his hand across his

chin. “I’m listening.”

“You are focusing on the early evening hours so I am thinking the killer used a fast-acting poison or a large dose.” Had she just pointed the finger of suspicion at Mrs. Browning?

“Have we considered monkshood?” Phillipa asked.

They all turned to look at her.

A quick glance at the detective suggested Phillipa had hit the nail on the head.

“Is it?” Evie asked.

“I will neither confirm nor deny it.”

Switching her attention to Phillipa, Evie asked, “Have we discussed monkshood?”

Phillipa didn’t think so. “I did some nighttime reading.” She closed her eyes as if trying to recall what she had learned. “Symptoms may appear almost immediately, sometimes no later than one hour. With large doses death is almost instantaneous or it can occur within two to six hours.” Phillipa opened her eyes again and looked at everyone for their reactions.

“What about the symptoms?” Evie asked her.

“They match the ones described by the detective and are almost similar to the symptoms suffered by foxglove poisoning.”

Evie gave the detective a pointed look. “Now will you confirm it?”

He sighed and nodded. “The medical examiner has finally provided definitive proof.”

“Detective. I don’t mean to tell you how to do

your job, however, is it possible the chauffeurs' version of events might not be entirely correct?"

He looked doubtful. "Are you suggesting they have been silenced?"

Evie lifted both shoulders. "I thought you didn't care for coincidences."

"They would have no reason to lie." He sat back. "Unless…"

Evie nodded. "They are employed by prominent families prepared to do everything within their power to prevent a scandal." Studying the pretty flower arrangement on the table, Evie also thought those families wouldn't necessarily share the information. If the chauffeurs had been silenced, they had acted independently. Or… the chauffeurs had simply been under strict orders from the victims to remain silent, no matter what.

"In their place, would you ask your staff to keep silent?" the detective asked.

"No. It is not my job to impede the efforts of the police. What's to be gained by that?" She didn't need to look at Tom to know he had rolled his eyes at her.

"Under any circumstance?" the detective asked.

Tom sat back and folded his arms. When his eyebrow curved up, Evie knew he shared the detective's curiosity and wanted to hear her response.

"You said it yourself, detective. Too many

coincidences become suspicious." She leaned forward and lowered her voice. "Those women did not go anywhere without their chauffeurs. What if… what if they were visiting someone who could ruin their reputations?"

"Would you feel better if I questioned the chauffeurs again? You seem to be suggesting I should."

Relaxing into her chair, she gave a casual shrug. "You are trying to map their whereabouts in the early evening. I am merely thinking someone is either lying or not telling the truth."

"You seem to think there is a difference."

Evie scoffed. "Of course there is."

The detective rested his arms on the table. "Have you ever refrained from telling the entire truth?"

She took care to mull over her answer, but before she could speak, Florence brought their pies.

"Will there be anything else?"

Everyone shook their heads.

They all waited for Florence to move away.

Feeling cornered, Evie spoke first, "Someone is lying. Either the chauffeurs or… Mrs. Browning. And someone is also doing their best to avoid telling the truth."

26

Waiting until they reached the edge of the village and they were well and truly out of earshot of the detective, Phillipa said, "Mrs. Browning is lying?"

A flock of birds took flight. Evie waited for their squawking to die down. "I had to give him something." She looked at Tom. "Before you say anything, I couldn't bring myself to mention Charlie Timms. Not now. The detective obviously spoke with him and put him in the clear. He has now moved on and is trying to fill in the gap between the time Mrs. Howard-Smith saw Charlie and then finally arrived home."

"Don't you think the detective would benefit from knowing both victims had been having an affair with him? It would widen his net of suspects. Remember those? You listed them. Also…"

"There's more?" Evie chirped.

"You failed to mention the doctor's maid."

Evie stopped. Throwing her head back, she

stared up at the sky. "Fine. Yes. I should have informed him…"

"Did Evie just agree with me?"

Grinning, Phillipa said, "I believe she did."

As a high-ranking member of the local community, she had responsibilities. What sort of example would she be setting by being deliberately evasive?

Evie swung around and broke off at a trot heading back toward the village. "Hurry. We might catch him before he leaves."

"I'm getting a feeling of déjà vu," Tom grumbled.

"Please don't push your luck," Evie warned. "I won't apologize for withholding information. I will not be reduced to playing the role of village gossip." Evie spent the rest of the way calling herself all types of fool. She had failed to recognize the clear distinction between spreading rumors and assisting an officer of the law to seek justice.

"Anyone would think you were infatuated with Charlie Timms."

Ignoring Tom's remark, Evie continued her mental rambling, thinking she had exercised full restraint for the wrong reasons and her worst crime had been failing to recognize it until now.

However, one simply did not go around propagating scandalous notions, certainly not the type which might bring into question everything she stood for. She frowned and tried to think exactly what that might be…

"I see his motor car," Phillipa said.

When Tom grabbed hold of Evie's arm, she came to an abrupt halt.

He surprised her by saying, "We might need to rethink this."

"Henrietta has already referred to us as Keystone Cops. I should like to avoid giving her reason for making the moniker stick."

"I'm not sure the detective will be pleased to find you have withheld information," Tom said. "He might hold you in some sort of contempt."

"I seem to remember saying that all along and, if I didn't, I most certainly should have mentioned it."

Phillipa said, "You could try to make an anonymous call."

"Too late. He's driven off." Evie swung back. Rolling her eyes, she said, "I wonder if I can disguise my voice on the telephone?"

***

Evie ended the call and sat back. "Happy now?"

Tom stretched his legs out and crossed them at the ankles. "Admit it. You feel better now that it's all out in the open. You can't possibly feel regrets."

"You're right. In fact, unburdening myself feels liberating. Perhaps now I can resume the task of settling into my new life in the country.

Henrietta will be pleased. I can now give the Hunt Ball my full attention."

"How did the detective react to your news?"

"Are you deliberately trying to derail my plans to put all this nasty business behind me?"

Tom sat up. "But the perpetrator hasn't been caught yet. I would have thought you'd want to follow up on it."

"In answer to your question, the detective didn't sound at all pleased about having to question Mrs. Browning again. He will also need to speak to her maid. Apparently, my line of questioning might have forced the information out of her so he needs to confirm it all." Savoring her new freedom, Evie searched for something to do. "I suppose I should have a word with Mrs. Horace about tonight's dinner and perhaps I should also start thinking about the rest of the month. It might be time to organize a house party." Striding to the fireplace, she rang the bell.

Edgar appeared momentarily.

"We should like tea in the library, Edgar. Could you let Miss Brady know, please? I believe she is with Caro."

When Tom picked up a newspaper, Evie found herself thinking this all felt rather anticlimactic. Selecting flowers for the upcoming Hunt Ball felt rather staid when compared to all the running around they had been doing.

A footman entered and organized the tea tray

on a table. Evie poured a cup and offered it to Tom.

"I'm beginning to acquire a taste for it. How long has it taken me?"

"Several months and you're even drinking it without cream."

"I thought the locals drank it only with milk."

"True." After several sips, she set her cup down and considered having a piece of lemon cake. Instead, she sat back and gazed out into the distance. "I wonder how the detective is getting on."

Tom chuckled. "It's only been a few minutes since you called him."

"I assume he will jump straight into it." She crossed her legs and swung her foot only to remember nanny always trying to break her of the habit. "I hope he hasn't dismissed my information as nonsensical. We spent a great deal of time digging around for it."

Phillipa entered the library and helped herself to some tea. "I think I got through to your maid. She might even consider trying a new hairstyle."

"Then, you have worked miracles. Did she rush off to the village to buy herself a new dress?"

"No, she said she had some work to do."

Evie couldn't think what that might be…

Unless…

No, surely Caro had put a stop to her sabotage.

"Did you happen to notice in which direction

she headed?"

"She said something about working on one of your hats which she had to fetch."

What could she possibly want to do to her hat? Sticks pins into it?

Dismissing the thought, she glanced at the telephone. Several minutes later, she found herself still looking at the telephone and the others had noticed.

"I know. I know. I'm obsessing." She nibbled on the tip of her thumb. "In one morning, we managed to gather more information than the detective. He should have done something with it and, as a gesture of goodwill, he should extend the courtesy and kept us informed."

Tom picked up his newspaper again and hid behind it while Phillipa helped herself to more cake.

"I'm inclined to agree with you," Phillipa said. "I rather enjoyed trekking out with you today."

Dismissing all the thoughts that had been plaguing her, Evie straightened. "You mentioned something about your friends organizing a treasure hunt. How exactly would that work?"

Phillipa looked down and smiled. "They're actually rather daring."

Tom lowered his newspaper and peered at her.

"I believe you have piqued Tom's interest and mine. So, you'll have to share more information."

"Well... in past treasure hunts, there have been items hidden within houses." She looked around her. "Large manor houses such as this one. For those not acquainted with the owners, this could prove somewhat problematic as they had to find ways into the house without breaking the law."

Tom set his newspaper aside.

"Would you, by any chance, happen to be here under false pretenses?" he asked.

Phillipa laughed. "Whatever do you mean?"

"I think Tom wants to know if your motor car really broke down?"

"Of course it did. Why would I fake that?"

"To gain entry into my house and hunt around for a mysterious object." Evie got up and refreshed her cup of tea. "What sort of objects are hidden?"

"Odd trinkets. Feathers. Silver spoons. If you put your mind to it, you can come up with the oddest objects."

"And, have you participated in one of these treasure hunts before?"

"This will be my first one. I do hope I can make it."

Taking the chair next to Tom, Evie asked, "Any suggestions as to how we can extricate the truth from Phillipa?"

"Do you think she's lying?"

"I'm not sure. If she is, she certainly knows how play her role. A part of me wishes to believe she has duped us."

"The bored part of you?" Tom asked. "Is that likely to become a problem in the future?"

"Are you afraid I'll find dangerous ways to keep myself entertained?"

"Considering how much you're fretting over the lack of news from the detective, yes, I am becoming seriously concerned."

Evie gave him an impish smile.

Phillipa cleared her throat. "I suddenly feel superfluous. Would you like me to leave?"

"Oh, no. I think I can turn this around and have some fun trying to figure out if you are telling the truth or not. In fact… Give me a moment. I have to think about this."

Evie got up and strode around the library, as she did, she looked at everything around her. A blue and white bowl filled with dried flowers. A collection of decorative snuff boxes. Candlesticks…

"You might have insinuated yourself into this household."

"To what end?" Phillipa asked.

"To gain inside knowledge. The first day I saw you at Mrs. Baker's Delights you produced a small flask and didn't have any qualms about pouring the contents into your cup."

"I wanted to… perk up my coffee."

Evie swung around to face Phillipa. "Did you have the opportunity to slip something into someone's cup?"

Shifting to the edge of her chair, Phillipa studied her for a moment. "I might have. I think you might be onto something." Phillipa clapped her hands. "This is fun. Let's play some more."

Slumping down on a chair, Evie cupped her chin in her hands. "I've lost the momentum." She looked over at the telephone. "He's not going to contact us."

"Once he catches the killer, he'll be busy extracting a confession," Tom said. "And, when he does, he will most likely transport the culprit to prison. But I'm sure he'll get around to paying you a visit and awarding you a medal."

Shaking her head, Evie strode over to the table. "More tea anyone? I'm feeling peckish, so I think I'll have more cake." Evie slid a slice onto a dainty plate.

Chortling, Phillipa asked, "Are you going to seek solace in a pound of cake?"

Evie smiled and took a sip of her tea only to stop. Looking up, she set the cup down on the saucer and heard it rattle. "Solace in food."

"What about it?" Tom asked.

"That's where Mrs. Browning and Mrs. Howard-Smith went…"

27

"Mrs. Penn said…" Evie clicked her fingers. "No, not Mrs. Penn but rather Mrs. Hallesberry, our second victim. Anyhow, she said there's something about the bereavement process that always stimulated her appetite."

Tom and Phillipa nodded.

"I think when Charlie Timms gave the victims their marching orders, they fell into a state of mourning for what they had lost."

This time only Phillipa nodded while Tom looked slightly skeptical.

"Have you never felt the loss of something and found comfort in food?" Evie asked.

Tom appeared to give it some thought.

Smiling, Phillipa said, "I don't think food would work on men. They would probably be inclined to rely on something stronger such as whiskey."

Tom gave a nod of understanding. "Oh, yes. That makes sense."

Phillipa surged to her feet and swirled around

the library. "I'm excited but I don't quite understand why."

Evie continued, "Heartbroken by Charlie Timms' decision to end the affair, Mrs. Howard-Smith went to see the doctor's wife. According to her maid, they then went out. On foot. Think about it. This is a small village so there is only one option."

"The pub," Tom suggested.

"But we know they didn't go there. It's a public place and not exactly the ideal milieu for ladies. If they had visited the pub, we would have heard about it."

Evie strode around the library and collected her thoughts. "So… We have been wondering where Mrs. Browning and Mrs. Howard-Smith went. As they traveled on foot, it would have to be somewhere close by."

Phillipa gasped. "Mrs. Baker's Delights?"

"That would be my guess."

Evie looked toward the mantle clock. "We have plenty of time to go into the village and return for dinner. We'll drive."

Phillipa looked crestfallen. "I suppose I'll hear all about it when you return."

"Nonsense. You can squash in with us."

Tom laughed. "No need. The roadster has a rumble seat."

"A what?" Phillipa asked.

"It's right where the luggage compartment should be. I think the British call it a dickey seat." He grinned. "Or a mother-in-law seat."

"I'll take either one if it means not missing out on the excitement." She looked at Evie. "I expect there will be excitement?"

Evie looked up at the ceiling and tried to picture the two women sneaking out of the house. It would have taken them five minutes to reach the tea room. But this would have been well after five in the afternoon.

"Florence!" Evie exclaimed. "She's not only the waitress, she is also the cook… And, now that I think about it, she also owns the business." Evie looked at Tom. "Do you remember we talked about it? Not at great length, but I do recall mentioning something about it."

He gave a pensive nod. "You were impressed by how much she had achieved for someone so young."

"I assume her establishment closes in the afternoon. That's probably when she does her baking."

Tom clasped his hands together. "You're trying to make the connection. By hook or by crook."

Where else would the doctor's wife have taken her guest? "It has to be the tea room. It won't hurt to ask." Evie hurried toward the fireplace and pulled the bell. When Edgar appeared, she said, "We are going to the village but should return in time for dinner."

Brushing both hands together, Tom said,

"That seems to have sealed the deal. I'll go prepare the roadster."

Striding out of the library, Phillipa mused, "Who comes up with those sorts of phrases? I know red tape comes from King Henry VIII's time. When he petitioned for a divorce, he had all his lords sign the document and that involved adding their seals with red ribbons attached."

"I think you just answered your own question," Evie said.

"Oh, seals." Phillipa tapped her chin. "Yes. It does make sense. Way back then, few people could write, including nobles, so they would sign papers by stamping them with their family seals."

"And how did you happen to know that?" Evie asked.

"Did I mention I grew up in the middle of nowhere? The nearest neighbors lived two days away and we had nothing but books for entertainment."

Settling into the rumble seat, Phillipa whooped. "This is going to be fun, I'm sure. Although, please try to avoid any bumps along the way. I wouldn't want to go flying."

The engine roared to life. Phillipa's laughter almost drowned it out. Getting into the spirit of it, Tom put his foot down and sent a shower of gravel spurting in their wake.

Along the way, they attracted the attention of a couple of maids making their way back to the house. Their surprise at seeing the Countess of Woodridge accompanied by a flamboyant looking passenger in the back seat waving her arms about, had them in stitches.

"I am supposed to set an example," Evie moaned. "Honestly, if this gets back to the dowagers, I shall never hear the end of it." Yet, Evie couldn't help smiling.

Reaching the village, Tom slowed down and found a spot for the motor car. "What's the plan?"

"We only want to gather information. Florence might not tell us straight out but she might say something to give herself away." Had Florence made concessions for the local committee ladies allowing them to enter her establishment after hours?

Tom brushed his hands along his face. "So, you're going to try to sweet talk her into giving you the information you need."

"You don't seem terribly excited by the idea."

Getting out of the roadster, Tom rounded the car, opened the passenger door and then gave Phillipa a hand.

"Oh, I'd planned on somehow swinging out of the back seat, but I suppose I should like to keep my neck intact."

On their previous trip to the village, Evie had been so focused on eluding the detective, she hadn't noticed if they'd drawn attention to themselves.

Despite trying to figure out how she could extract the information she needed out of Florence, she managed to pay attention and saw several people turning to glance their way.

They walked past the vicarage and saw Mrs. Ellington collecting flowers from the garden. Evie thought they should have pointed the finger of suspicion and named the Vicar's wife as the third committee lady having an affair with Charlie Timms if only to give her a bit of make-believe excitement. She had been rather thrilled by the sight of the local Lothario. So, Evie didn't think there would have been any harm in it.

As they neared the doctor's house, Evie gave Tom's sleeve a tug and grabbed hold of Phillipa's hand telling them both to step it up. The detective's motor car sat outside the doctor's house. He had either gone in to speak with Mrs. Browning or…

Evie looked around them.

No sight of him. For all she knew, Mrs. Browning might have told him she and Mrs. Howard-Smith had gone to Florence's tea room.

They would soon find out.

"Are we going to pretend we are returning for more pie?" Tom asked.

"Oh, I hadn't thought about that." They couldn't really go into the tea room claiming to have some questions for Florence regarding the death of a couple of committee members. Evie patted her stomach. "As much as I love her pies,

I'm not sure I can fit another one in."

Glancing at Tom, she saw him patting his stomach too.

"No, nor could I. We could purchase some pies to take with us. It's the least we can do considering we're going into her tea room under false pretenses…"

When they reached the tea room, they peered through the window. There were several customers enjoying afternoon tea and scones.

"They look good," Evie murmured.

Florence emerged from the back room carrying a tray.

"She looks run off her feet," Phillipa observed. "How old do you think she is?"

"No older than twenty-five. That's my guess." How had someone so young managed to finance her business venture?

Phillipa must have pondered the same question. "Perhaps I should do something worthwhile with my small inheritance."

"Isn't that what you are doing?" Evie asked.

"Having a good time so I can then write about it?" Phillipa laughed. "She must have a good head on her shoulders. I suppose we're all gifted different talents."

Yes, and Florence appeared to have more than her share since she did her own baking and seemed to manage her finances well enough to bide her time before hiring someone.

Evie thought she remembered Henrietta

mentioning one of her butlers had retired from service and had set up his own tea room but that had been after many years in service. Clearly enough time for him to accumulate the funds necessary to open a business.

At twenty-five, Florence might have had a couple of years' experience working elsewhere but not many. Certainly not enough to have been able to put aside a bundle of money.

"Your frown is becoming progressively more serious," Phillipa remarked.

"I'm now wondering where she came from. She must have a family. If she's not from around here, why did she choose this village?"

Lowering her voice, Phillipa said, "To get away from a dark past."

Evie stopped blinking. She knew Phillipa had merely filled in the blank but what if she had also inadvertently stumbled on the truth?

"Are we going in?" Tom asked.

"Someone is becoming impatient," Evie whispered. "Yes, let's go in and interrogate our unsuspecting victim."

Rushing past them, Florence smiled and said, "I'll be with you shortly."

"Take your time," Evie encouraged. Exchanging looks with the others, she lifted her shoulders into a shrug. Now what? How could they engage Florence in conversation when she seemed so run off her feet?

Phillipa sidled up to her and whispered,

"Should we get a table?"

They'd already decided that would look too odd. A moment later, Florence emerged from the back room wiping her hands on her apron.

"You appear to be quite busy," Evie said.

"I had some pies that needed to come out of the oven. Would you like me to show you to a table?"

"Oh… No, we… we actually wanted to take some pies with us."

Smiling, Florence directed her attention to the pies on display. "Which one would you like?"

"I think we might try something different. I'll let you decide."

"How many would you like?"

Ridden with guilt by her underhandedness, Evie said, "We'll take a dozen. No, make that two dozen. It would be a lovely treat for the house staff."

As Florence collected the pies, Evie congratulated herself. It would take some time to wrap all those pies giving them the opportunity to ask a few essential questions.

If only one would come to mind…

"I keep forgetting to ask what time you close for the day."

"There's a sign on the front door. I try to finish up at five in the afternoon but that doesn't always work out."

"Oh? Do you have people lingering over your fine pies?"

Florence gave her a brisk smile. “Sometimes.”

Evie needed to find a way to ask about Mrs. Browning and Mrs. Howard-Smith without sounding too desperate for the information. “I thought you might have been opened until much later. I seem to recall someone saying they had enjoyed a lovely dinner here.”

“Yes,” Phillipa piped in. “I heard Mrs. Browning say so.”

Studying Florence’s reaction, Evie thought she detected a slight twitch of her lip. Had mention of Mrs. Browning hit a raw nerve?

“Will you be carrying these with you or would you like me to organize delivery?”

If Evie had to decipher her response, she’d say that had been a deliberate attempt at evasion.

“Yes, we’ll take them with us, please.” Scooping in a breath, she continued, “Mrs. Browning has been a strong supporter of your establishment.”

“That is mighty nice of the lady.”

“You have certainly won our support. I have been craving these pies at all hours. I wonder… What would happen if I came knocking on your door in the early evening?”

Florence wiped her hands on her apron and gave her a tight smile. “If I’m still baking, I’ll probably open the door. I’m not one to turn my nose up at another sale.” Her gaze shifted to the door.

Turning, Evie saw the detective enter. Had he

come for the pies or to ask Florence some questions?

With her purchases all parceled up, Evie would have to concoct an excuse to linger. She saw Tom dig inside his pocket. Producing a wallet, he paid for the pies. Something Evie hadn't expected so she made a mental note to reimburse him for the expense.

"Will there be anything else, milady?"

Giving a small shake of her head, Evie turned slightly and greeted the detective. "Back for more pie, detective?"

"I would like a word with Miss Florence Green."

"Certainly, sir. I will just be a moment. I need to check my oven."

As Florence retreated into the back room, Evie distributed the parcels so they could carry them to the roadster. Leaning toward the detective, she whispered, "We should like to have a word with you once you are finished here."

"Are we leaving?" Phillipa whispered. "But we didn't get what we came for?"

The detective must have heard her. His eyebrows hitched up. "You have your pies. What else did you come for?"

"Oh… We'll explain later." She hoped their next encounter didn't come too soon. Evie needed some time to figure out what this all meant...

28

"We have a slight problem." Tom nudged his head toward the roadster. "Where do we put all these pies?"

Evie looked up and down the street.

Tom smiled. "Are you feeling a little lost without your bell?"

"Are you suggesting I cannot function without servants?" Liftin her chin, she strode off.

"Are you going off in a huff or do you want us to follow you?" Tom asked.

Resting her chin on the stack of pies, Evie said, "You can stand there if you like but I'm going to take these pies to Henrietta's house. She should be able to keep them safe for us."

The dowager's house came into view and not a moment too soon. Evie stopped because if she took another step, she would have pies scattered all around her. Her hands ached, her arms shook. Who would have thought a few pies would weigh so much?

Tom and Phillipa caught up with her and walked right past her, their steps even and slow. Evie realized her mistake had been in walking too quickly.

"You could set the pies down and I'll collect them later," Tom called out.

"If you can do it, I can do it too," she found herself muttering under her breath.

Evie reached the dower house just as a footman approached her.

"I'll take those, milady."

Evie could barely draw enough breath to thank the footman. Straightening her jacket, she pressed on and reached the front steps with only one thought in mind. "Tea."

Tom and Phillipa had also been relieved of their burdens and had waited for Evie to arrive.

"Very kind of you, but, in your place, I would have gone straight in."

"Well," Phillipa exclaimed in jest, "we'll keep that in mind."

Half way along the hallway, Evie heard the dowager.

"Bradley, what is that commotion I hear?"

"I barely made a sound," Evie said as she strode into the front parlor and headed straight for a chair.

Henrietta looked at Tom and Phillipa. "What have you done to poor Evangeline? She looks as though she's taking her last breath."

"We brought pies," Evie said.

"Whatever for and why are you slumping and breathing so hard?"

"Long story. May we please have some tea?" Evie straightened and inspected her hands. She would definitely look into taking up gardening. Perhaps she could carry a full bucket around as exercise. The stack of pies had been up to her chin, but she hadn't realized they would become such a heavy burden after only a few steps.

Evie frowned and sat up.

When they'd arrived at Mrs. Baker's Delights, Florence had just taken some pies out of the oven. Yet, when the detective said he wanted to speak with her, she asked for a moment because she needed to check her oven…

Just as Henrietta instructed the butler to bring refreshments, the sound of a whistle blowing had them all standing up and rushing to the window.

"What on earth could that be?" Evie gasped.

"It's the local constable blowing his whistle," Henrietta said. "Although, why he has done so is beyond me. This is a quiet little village inhabited by law abiding citizens."

"Henrietta, you seem to forget the two recent murders."

Henrietta glanced at Evie. "Has anyone actually verified that as a fact?"

"Well, the police are looking into the deaths." And they had been curious enough to run around the place interviewing people.

"Here is a theory I'm sure no one has thought about." Henrietta drew everyone's attention to her. "What if Mrs. Hallesberry poisoned Mrs. Howard-Smith and then decided she couldn't live with her crime and so took her own life."

They all tilted their heads and stared at Henrietta with more than a hint of awe reflected in their eyes.

The dowager smiled. "You'd think I had just revealed a universal secret. When, in fact, it is nothing but a supposition that could have occurred to anyone."

"It's quite humbling to hear you say so," Evie remarked. "If I'd come up with that theory, let me assure you, I would have shouted it from the rooftops. It sounds feasible enough to warrant another chat with the detective."

Hurried footsteps approached and Sara entered the drawing room. "What on earth is going on?"

"We're all asking ourselves the same question, Sara. You'd think our peaceful little village had come under siege. Everyone is running around like headless chooks."

"Surely, you exaggerate." Sara strode up to the window.

They all stood on tiptoes and looked toward the main street in the village. People were indeed running about but most stood by craning their necks to catch sight of the commotion.

"I suggest sending Mr. Winchester out to

investigate. I do not dare set foot outside this house until order has been restored."

Tom had already moved toward the door and as Henrietta drew in a breath, he stepped out.

They saw him break into a trot and move toward the end of the street.

The whistle blew again startling Sara who stood with her hand pressed against her chest.

Without moving away from the window, Henrietta said, "You were going to tell me about the pies and your reason for looking so winded."

Evie told her about her theory. Although, in her opinion, it paled in comparison to the theory proposed by Henrietta.

"You think they went in there after the store closed and drowned their sorrows with pie?" Henrietta's eyes brimmed with amusement. "Why would Mrs. Browning do that? Had she been having an affair too?"

"Not that we know of. Perhaps she wanted to stand by her friend… as a sign of sisterly solidarity."

Phillipa nodded. "I would certainly offer a shoulder to cry on, especially if it meant sharing some of your delicious pies."

"What is the fixation with these pies I have been hearing so much about?" Henrietta asked.

"You haven't tried them?"

"I have a cook. Why would I purchase my food somewhere else?"

"Not everyone has a cook and… the wheels of

change are in motion. More and more women wish to have a respite from their daily duties or they simply don't have the skills to make everything."

Henrietta could not have looked more puzzled.

"Is it a fine eating establishment?"

"Are you saying you haven't even set foot inside?"

"Don't look at me as if I have grown an extra head. I have eaten in restaurants. In fact, only last month I dined at the Ritz. You should know that since you were there."

"Not everyone can dine at the Ritz, Henrietta."

The dowager made a series of gestures that both amused and puzzled Evie. A simple dismissive wave of her hand would have sufficed but the dowager had thrown in a roll of her eyes, the slight pursing of her lips…

Finally, Henrietta continued, "You were telling us about your theory and some sort of cure for heartbreak and I'm sure you were about to make a third point. Perhaps you were about to mention Mrs. Hallesberry?"

Third person.

Evie thought back to the first time she had gone into Florence's tea room. Everyone had been agog at the sight of Charlie Timms.

Had Florence been among the admirers?

Nibbling on the edge of her lip, she looked out

of the window. "Somewhere along the line, it occurred to me that there might be someone prepared to get rid of their competition." She knew Florence had met Charlie Timms because she'd seen him eating one of her pies. They were delivered to him…

Did Florence personally deliver the pies?

"I think I found our third person."

The whistle blew again.

"You appear to be doing better than the constable who is clearly still trying to find one person."

She played around with a scenario. The two women sought refuge in the tea room. Florence overheard their conversation. As she prepared the pies, she gave particular attention to one of them.

Had Mrs. Hallesberry suffered the same fate? Had she sought out a friendly ear, visiting the doctor's wife who then took her to the tea room where she knew they could have the place to themselves?

She saw Tom hurrying up the path. When he entered the drawing room, she stepped forward to tell him about her new theory but he beat her to it.

"Florence has made a run for it."

29

The whole art of war consists of guessing at what is on the other side of the hill.
- Duke of Wellington

Evie rushed toward the door only to stop at the hard command issued by Henrietta.

"Evangeline Halton, Countess of Woodridge, I forbid you to step outside this house. If anything were to happen to you, Nicholas would never forgive me and I will not enter the kingdom of heaven with the heavy burden of guilt."

Hiding her smile, Evie turned, "Who says you're going to heaven?"

Henrietta lifted her chin a notch. "You have been warned. And the same goes for anyone else thinking of putting their life in peril. I will not have that on my conscience."

"Strictly speaking," Evie said, "we are not thinking of rushing out there for your sake. Although, we would like to see peace restored in your village. Otherwise, I'm sure you'll never find a moment's rest."

"Fine, be a fool and rush out there."

Evie turned only to stop again. This time, because Tom's hand had wrapped around her arm. "Where do you think you're going? I have a real person to answer to. If anything were to happen to you, your grandmother would have me strung up and staked to an ant hill."

"Have some tea," Henrietta offered.

Phillipa edged toward the door.

"Don't you dare. If I can't go out there, neither can you. If anything happens to you, I will be the one burdened with the task of informing your parents."

They all looked at Tom. "Well, what are you waiting for? Go out there and get us some more news."

"So much for my life of adventure," Phillipa complained.

"Have some pie," Evie offered.

"I don't dare. I've been thinking…"

As they waited for Tom to return, Phillipa told them about the theory she had been working on.

"That is so odd," Evie said. "I reached the same conclusion. Now it will be up to the detective to confirm it or deny it." Accepting a cup of tea, Evie lifted it to her lip only to set it down. "Remember what you said earlier about Florence having a dark past? I thought you might have been joking. Now, I think you might have been right…"

"Do you think she is a poisoner?"

Evie had wanted to give Charlie Timms the benefit of the doubt. At one point, she had wondered if she had fallen under his charm.

"Did you see the way she reacted when the detective came in?" Evie asked. Had she heard him say he wanted to ask her some questions? "She probably thought the jig was up and so decided to make a run for it."

"I think I see Tom returning." Phillipa stood on her toes. "Yes. It's him."

Evie saw Henrietta breathe a sigh of relief. Had she really been concerned for everyone's safety? Of course, she had been right to recommend being cautious…

"She's been caught," Tom said as he entered.

Evie handed him a cup of tea and saw him weighing the cup as if wondering if he could have something stronger.

"Now what?" she asked. "Will the detective take her into custody? She more or less gave herself away by fleeing."

"That's my guess too. I imagine we'll be hearing from the detective. He does owe you a debt of gratitude. After all, you pointed him in the right direction."

"Are you praising me?"

"I'm awarding credit where it is due."

They all talked at once. Questions and answers and more suppositions crisscrossed the drawing room.

Sara strode out only to return to the drawing

room. "Why are there so many pies lined up on every available surface in the hallway?"

***

Evie eyed the beaded dress Caro held up for her and wondered what would happen when she stepped into it.

"Would you prefer another dress?" Caro asked.

It's only a dress, Evie told herself. Holding her breath, she stepped into it. When the beads stayed in place, she relaxed.

Earlier, she had been prepared to rush out into danger, something she would never have considered doing in her life.

What had come over her?

When Phillipa had told her about the car rally, Evie had felt as though she had been missing out. She wanted to remain living at Halton House but how much would she be missing out on? Life appeared to be moving at tremendous speed. What if it left her behind?

"Caro, have you been enjoying your time in Berkshire?" Her maid worked every day, but unlike the other servants, she had more freedom to come and go.

"I had been, yes."

"Has something changed now?"

Caro went through the process of selecting a headdress for Evie. "I don't dare go into the village now in case I bump into Charlie Timms."

Had word got out about his affairs?

So soon?

It had only been a few hours since Florence had been captured by the police. Even if she had confessed to everything, the police would not have made the information public.

"Rumor has it, he and Elizabeth Young have an agreement."

"That sounds rather old-fashioned." As opposed to what? Evie wondered. An affair?

"They were seen going to the pub for dinner."

"When?"

"Only a short while ago."

Evie couldn't hide her surprise. "And you already know about it?"

"One of the footman had been enjoying his half day off. He was making his way back to the house when he saw them. So… I suppose that's that. I have missed my chance."

"But you mustn't give up hope." Privately, Evie breathed a sigh of relief. She might have been in favor of Charlie Timms' innocence, but the man was a bit of a rascal and certainly not good enough for Caro. Then again, Elizabeth Young had agreed to be seen in public with him. Had she discovered something about him others didn't know? Living next door, she would have access to a different side to him. Maybe he had turned a new leaf… Evie hoped he had, for Elizabeth's sake.

Caro adjusted a feather on Evie's hair and gave it a little tug as if to show Evie she didn't have any tricks up her sleeve today.

Regardless, Evie wouldn't drop her guard. She stood in front of the mirror and gave the dress a few discreet tugs to make sure it wouldn't come undone at the seams.

Out of the corner of her eye, she thought she saw Caro smiling. Maybe this is what she planned, Evie thought, feeling on tenterhooks and about to jump out of her skin.

"Is something wrong, milady?"

"Nothing at all, Caro." She selected a fragrance. Normally, she dabbed it on without thinking. This time, she uncapped it and took a tentative whiff of it. "I think I'm as ready as I will ever be. Unless…"

"Unless what, milady?"

"Nothing." She took her time walking to the door. When she reached it, she tested the door handle. It opened with ease.

"Have a good evening, Caro."

Taking the stairs down to the drawing room, she kept her attention fixed on every step she took only to laugh. What did she expect would happen? The stairs to crumble beneath her? The floor to collapse from under her?

By the time she reached the bottom of the stairs, she convinced herself Caro had ended her siege.

Entering the drawing room, she heard

Henrietta chatting with Tom.

"My butler's brother emigrated to America last summer. He is quite taken with the country and all its oddities. Imagine my surprise when I heard he had fully embraced the game… He wrote in great detail about one of your players, Babe Ruth. Apparently, he single-handedly—"

Evie gasped. "Henrietta and Sara. How lovely it is to see you both."

"Anyone would think you haven't seen us in years when it's only been a few hours."

"Phillipa. What a lovely ensemble. Don't you agree, Sara?" She couldn't believe Henrietta, of all people, had been talking with Tom about baseball.

"Evangeline, I never did ask if you follow any of those baseball teams…"

Evie looked away. "Does everyone have a drink. Edgar? Yes, I see you've taken care of everyone." Evie sat down next to Phillipa only to jump to her feet again. "Any news from the detective?"

They all stared at Evie with a hint of wariness.

"I think today's excitement has been too much for Evangeline," Henrietta whispered.

"I for one feel hard done by," Phillipa said. "I've never seen anyone being arrested."

Henrietta held her glass close to her mouth. "And why would you want to?"

"To gain life experience, of course."

"Phillipa wishes to become a writer,

Henrietta. That's why she came to England," Evie explained.

"But you have writers in the Antipodes." Henrietta glanced at Sara. "Who is that author you are reading at the moment?"

"Miles Franklin," Sara replied. "I'm thoroughly enjoying My Brilliant Career."

"If you haven't read her book, I'm sure Sara will be only too happy to lend it to you."

Edgar strode to the door and spoke to a footman. Turning, he announced, "Detective Inspector O'Neill."

Evie swung around, happy for some news but quite ecstatic to have the conversation about baseball interrupted.

"Detective."

"My apologies for intruding at such an hour, my lady."

"Please, join us. In fact, we are going in soon. Would you care to join us for dinner? I won't take no for an answer."

"I'm… I'm not dressed for it, my lady."

"We don't mind, but we would mind if you left us in the dark. I take it you came here to share some news?"

"Yes, indeed, I have. But it might not actually be a suitable subject for the dinner table."

"After everything that's happened, I think our sensitivities can withstand a shock or two."

"It's about Miss Florence Green. If you recall, she excused herself to check the oven just as you were leaving the premises. When several minutes passed and she still hadn't come out, I looked in the back room and found it empty."

Evie nodded. "We heard she had taken off."

"Yes, she tried to evade us, but we caught up with her. It took some doing and eventually we got a confession out of her."

Everyone leaned forward.

"She poisoned both victims."

Confirmation of what they already knew had everyone gaping.

"Did she give a reason?" Evie asked.

"Jealousy. She said it tore her apart to see the victims with her man."

Florence Green had been the third person?

"We have reason to believe she suffers from delusions," the detective added.

"What does that mean?" Henrietta asked.

"She believed herself to be in love with Mr. Timms. She also believed he had encouraged her."

"So… it was all in her imagination?" Evie asked.

The detective nodded.

Heavens. She would never again complain about Caro. Her maid had been infatuated with Charlie Timms, but now that she knew he had paired up with Elizabeth Young, Caro was sensible enough to put it all behind her.

Turning to Evie, the detective smiled. "It's not often a member of the public proves to be of use to the police. We… we appreciate your input, Lady Woodridge." His smile brightened. "With your assistance, we were able to capture a woman who had eluded the police for quite some time."

Sara and Henrietta exclaimed, "Really?"

He pushed out a long breath. "She originally hails from Birmingham. She married quite young and her husband was over fifteen years older. He owned a store and did quite well for himself. Then, one day, he collapsed and died. Miss Green had been slowly feeding him poison. We believe she had been planning it for a long while. Before anyone became suspicious, she fled."

Henrietta collapsed into her chair. "All this time, a poisoner had been living among us?"

A poisoner who happened to bake the most delectable pies Evie had ever tasted.

"Out of curiosity, did the doctor's wife prove to be at all useful?" Evie asked.

The detective gave a pensive nod. "It took some doing but she finally broke down and told me how she and Mrs. Howard-Smith had been in need of what they referred to as comfort food. She wouldn't tell me why but she also revealed doing the same with Mrs. Hallesberry."

It surprised Evie to learn Mrs. Browning had not revealed anything about the affairs. Evidently, keeping it secret had been more important than helping to catch a killer.

To think Florence Green had been the one to

hold the strongest objections to the affairs…

Looking up, she saw Edgar enter the drawing room. He stood at attention and gave a nod.

Smiling, Evie announced, “Dinner is served.”

Epilogue

All's well that ends well
- William Shakespeare

Evie looked up from her teacup and studied her butler. Edgar stood by the buffet table dressed in his smart suit and looking quite pleased with himself. Setting her cup down, she shuffled through the small stack of letters and found the one she had been expecting. Opening it, she inspected the contents and smiled.

"Edgar."

He stepped forward. "Yes, my lady."

"Are you fond of the theater?" She needn't have asked since Caro had already confirmed it, stating with absolute certainty Edgar harbored a true passion for the theater.

"As a matter of fact, I am, my lady."

"I'm so glad to hear you say so. I have been trying to think of a way to express my gratitude. You have been ever so patient, filling in while Mr. Crawford visited his sister."

"I have been only too happy to help out."

"In any case, I have secured a couple of tickets to a show. It's called The Unknown and it's playing at the Aldwych in London. I thought you might like them." Evie handed him the tickets and watched his eyes sparkle with excitement.

"For me?"

"Yes. I hope you enjoy the performance. I believe Basil Rathbone is playing a lead role."

Edgar held the tickets as if he were cradling something precious. Bowing slightly, he resumed his post by the buffet table.

One problem solved, Evie thought. Hopefully, the tickets would soften the blow. She suspected Mr. Crawford would soon be announcing his retirement, leaving her with no butler at Halton House. She could either employ someone new or… she could talk Edgar into staying on in the country instead of heading back to town.

Setting the letters aside, she turned her attention to her breakfast. A moment later, Phillipa joined her.

"My motor car has been fixed."

"Oh, does this mean you will leave us?" An odd sensation swirled around her throat. Yes, she would definitely miss Phillipa.

"I'm afraid so."

"Needless to say, I will welcome you back at any time," Evie said. "After the adventure we shared, I believe you have earned a special place in our lives." Evie picked up her teacup only to set it down again. When had she started referring to herself in the plural?

Tom strode in and greeted them.

"Does the pub not offer breakfast?" Evie asked.

"I prefer your spread."

Phillipa clapped her hands. "I just remembered. I contacted one of the people I will be meeting at the car rally. One of his friends is from your neck of the woods and he told me they had been celebrating. So, I've been meaning to congratulate you on your win. I hear the New York Yankees performed extremely well—"

Evie succumbed to a fit of coughing prompting Phillipa to jump to her feet and rush to pat her on the back.

"Oh, heavens. My tea must have gone down the wrong way. Thank you, Phillipa."

"Are you sure you're fine?"

"Yes. Thank you."

Tom set down his plate and sat opposite Evie. "Phillipa. I believe you can rest easy. Sit down and have your breakfast. The Countess will be fine. She is only concerned about you hurting my feelings."

"Really? How?" Phillipa asked.

"I believe you were about to say the Yankees had trounced the Red Sox."

"Oh, I see I'm late with the news. When did you hear about it?"

Tom dug inside his pocket and produced the telegram he had received. "News about it arrived several days ago. But I think Evie received the news first. Clearly, she is better connected."

Evie gasped. "You knew."

"If you both knew," Phillipa said, "and neither one mentioned it…" Shaking her head, she finished by saying, "I am definitely missing something."

Tom winked at her. "I'm a Red Sox fan and Evie here happens to be a Yankees fan."

Phillipa turned to her. "Oh, then it's you I should be congratulating."

"I didn't want to make a fuss…"

Tom laughed. "What made you change your mind? A while back you gave me the impression you would have a field day at my expense."

Phillipa smiled. "I think you're right. Evie wanted to spare your feelings."

Tom held her gaze.

Evie felt a flush of heat settle on her cheeks. "Nonsense. I merely wanted to choose the right moment to tease you."

Edgar cleared his throat and announced, "Lady Woodridge."

Henrietta hurried into the dining room. "Oh, I see I'm in time for a second breakfast. We have such a busy day ahead of us."

"We do?" Evie asked.

"The Hunt Ball, my dear. Time is of the essence. We only have a month or so to get everything right. And, before that, we have to attend Mrs. Hallesberry's funeral." Henrietta shook her head. "Since the killer has been caught, this one should be a breeze. I have saved the best until last. According to my butler who heard it from one of his many admirers…" Henrietta waved her hand. "I have lost track of which one… never mind."

Evie smiled. "What did you hear?"

"Oh… One of your tenants is getting married. Charlie Timms has finally decided to settle down. I believe there will be many hearts broken. But all is well and we will get to toast someone's health."

Edgar poured the dowager some tea.

"Now, what have I missed?" Henrietta asked.

"Phillipa is about to bid us farewell."

"I must say, your visit has been quite refreshing." Henrietta looked at Tom. "I suppose you will soon be moving on."

Oh dear…

The complication Evie had expected had finally reared its ugly head. How would Mr. Tom Winchester transform himself into her chauffeur now?

"Not for a while," Evie said. "Tom is going to help me find a new chauffeur." That would take care of the immediate future, but what on earth would they do after that? How would Tom justify staying around…?

"I hadn't realized you were without a chauffeur," Henrietta murmured.

"Yes, I lost him recently. He… went in search of greener pastures."

"Greener than the ones you offered?"

Henrietta sounded affronted.

Floundering for a response, Evie looked at Tom but he merely raised his eyebrow.

"Yes, since you put it that way. I shall have to choose my next chauffeur with greater care…"

Evie gazed out toward the gardens and wondered how she could justify keeping Tom around. When Henrietta drew her attention to the Hunt Ball, Evie decided to postpone making any decisions. In any case, this had been Tom's doing so he should provide her with a solution.

"Are you listening, Evie?"

"Yes, of course," Evie said and turned her full attention to the here and now leaving everything else for another day.

*****

Author Notes
Facts and Historical references

In my effort to ensure the story remained historically correct, I spent many hours checking and double-checking word and phrase usage. Here are some examples:

Week-end: 1630s, from week + end. Originally a northern word (referring to the period from Saturday noon to Monday morning); it became general after 1878.

Getaway: 1852, "an escape," originally in fox hunting, from verbal phrase get away "escape". Of prisoners or criminals from 1893.

Pot-hole: 1826, originally a geological feature in glaciers and gravel beds. Applied to a hole in a road from 1909.

Like a bat out of hell: The Lions of the Lord: A Tale of the Old West By Harry Leon Wilson, Copyright 1903, published June, 1903, page 107 (google book full view):

Why, I tell you, young man, if I knew any places where the pinches was at, you'd see me comin' the other way like a bat out of hell.

Come clean: Moberly Evening Democrat, August 1904

Rain check: First recorded in 1880-1885

By hook or by crook: The phrase is very old, first recorded in 1380

Also…

Baseball

May 1, 1920: Babe Ruth's first Yankee home run is a 'colossal clout' against Red Sox. As the second month of the 1920 season opened, the New York Yankees routed the Boston Red Sox at the Polo Grounds, 6-0, behind Babe Ruth's first home run as a New Yorker.

Printed in Poland
by Amazon Fulfillment
Poland Sp. z o.o., Wrocław